MW00564705

Praise for *Gordon B. Haunting Weird Horror(s)*

Ranging from the uncanny to the haunting to the horrific, Gordon B. White's stories take what you think of you know of Horror and the Weird and give it one extra torque, one additional turn, opening the portal out of the real that much wider. These are stunning and provocative stories, full of surprises.

— Brian Evenson, author of *The Glassy Burning Floor of Hell*

What impresses me most about White's writing is the near-boundless risk-taking inherent within. He consistently pushes boundaries of form and genre in a way that's exhilarating, and *Gordon B. White is creating...* continues that fearlessness. Absolutely one of my favorite horror authors working today; I'll read whatever he writes.

— Keith Rosson, author of *Fever House*

Literary anatomists will discover the DNA of Ambrose Bierce and Algernon Blackwood ingrained within these tales, but what will really take their breath away—and yours, dear reader—are the genetic strands of a bold new voice in contemporary horror. The fifteen specimens that comprise this harrowing collection is scientific proof that Gordon B. White is in a genre-genus by himself, unclassifiable, breathtaking and beautiful all at once.

— Clay McLeod Chapman, author of *Ghost Eaters*

In his latest collection, Gordon B. White's haunting and lyrical prose is so rich, so captivating and immersive that I'm utterly convinced that the words on the page are watching me—vigilant eyes peering through the curve of each printed letter and beckoning me to wander further into the soul-devouring, all-consuming void.

— Eric LaRocca, author of *Things Have Gotten Worse*
Since We Last Spoke

Gordon B. White is creating Haunting Weird Horror(s)

Gordon B. White

TREPIDATIO

PUBLISHING

Copyright 2023 © Gordon B. White

All rights reserved. No part of this book may be used or reproduced by any means, graphic, electronic, or mechanical, including photocopying, recording, taping or by any information storage retrieval system without the written permission of the publisher except in the case of brief quotations embodied in critical articles and reviews.

This is a work of fiction. All of the characters, names, incidents, organizations, and dialogue in this novel are either the products of the author's imagination or are used fictitiously.

The views expressed in this work are solely those of the authors and do not necessarily reflect the views of the publisher, and the publisher hereby disclaims any responsibility for them.

ISBN: 978-1-68510-094-0 (sc)
ISBN: 978-1-68510-095-7 (ebook)
Library of Congress Control Number: 2023936761

First printing edition: October 13, 2023
Printed by Trepidatio Publishing in the United States of America
Cover Design, Cover Layout, & Interior Layout: Gordon B. White
Edited by Sean Leonard
Proofread by Scarlett R. Algee
Cover Image: *An unconscious naked man lying on a table being attacked by little demons armed with surgical instruments; representing the effects of chloroform on the human body.* Watercolor by R. Cooper. Wellcome Collection. Attribution 4.0 International (CC BY 4.0) (alterations made).

Trepidatio Publishing, an imprint of JournalStone Publishing
3205 Sassafras Trail
Carbondale, Illinois 62901

Trepidatio books may be ordered through booksellers or by contacting:

JournalStone | www.journalstone.com

For my mom, Mary, who let me stay up far too late reading things I probably shouldn't have

Contents

Gordon B. White is creating Haunting Weird Horror

You've enjoyed a few of his stories and you follow each other on Twitter, so when you see that horror and weird fiction author Gordon B. White has started a Patreon, you think, "Sure, I'll throw him a couple of bucks." You pick the $7 tier—*Postcards of Lesser-Known Haunted Houses*—thinking it might be a lark to get a picture and a microfiction each month for your modest contribution.

You missed the first month's mail drop, but it's just $7. In fact, you've forgotten about it until the next month, on the thirteenth, when your first perk arrives: a 3 1/2 x 5 postcard, postmarked in Seattle with a Forever stamp from the USPS's Spooky Silhouettes line, this one with happy and sad drama mask ghosts framed in orange foil windows. It's kitschy, but the picture on the front is just a normal house.

Craftsman-style, one story. Blue siding, red door, white curtains. The picture was taken at dusk, but the walkway lights give it a vibrance. In a cramped hand in blue ink, the back reads:

1247 Sawtuck Road. *Haunted by a boy with the face of a stillborn Janus kitten and scissor blades protruding from under his eyelids. When he cries, he goes snip-snip. He is more often heard than seen, but whisker clippings are common in dusty corners or matted into unattended hairbrushes.*

That's it. Not without its creepy charm, but for $7? Inside, you leave it in the mail pile with the bank statements and explanations of benefits that you tell yourself you'll read but will really just throw away next month. You forget about it there—the postcard, the boy with the kitten faces—but that night you wake from dreams of soft blade sounds and the sensation of thick hairs falling across your face.

Next month, on the thirteenth, the second postcard comes. The house on the front is two stories, boxy, with Tudor-style trim. The lawn is unkempt and a pink bicycle with training wheels is lodged in the hedges. Why, you wonder, would someone leave it like that if they were having a photo taken?

329 Mantooth Dr. *A ghost of a bird resides in the attic; a ghost of a mouse in the pantry. A little girl with a mouth like a dripping bloom of wilted carnations hunts them from three a.m. until dawn. She doesn't like to be looked at.*

Preposterous. What are these, repurposed Tweets? Still, when you take it inside to throw it away—along with the card about the whisker clipping ghost—you can't find the previous one. You set down 329 Mantooth to look through the pile, but when you turn back, the new postcard is gone too. All night, you are sure you hear scratching in the cabinets, and when you wake up in the morning, you catch the hint of a sweet smell that could be flowers or rotting meat or just your imagination.

You cancel your Patreon pledge. You're not scared, of course, but these dribbles aren't worth $7. That's the reason: value. And when you go to unfollow Gordon B. White on Twitter, only to find that his account seems to have blocked you and his DMs are closed? Well, that just proves you were right. There's nothing worse than an "artist" who doesn't take at least some small personal interest in his followers.

But next month, sure as the full moon, the thirteenth arrives and with it a postcard of an old Victorian, crumbling outside, the photo taken from behind rusted gates.

14 Continental. *The final owner left three severed heads from bearded men on a closet shelf, radio speakers in each one's mouth. They've never made a sound, but sometimes they appear in inappropriate places, eyes rolling left* *to right like a dial. The refrigerator is a typical hiding spot on hot days, the oven on cold.*

You throw this one in the trash outside, but even so, you hesitate before opening your appliances to make dinner. Instead, you order out for Thai. While you wait for the delivery, you contact Patreon support and also confirm with your credit card company that the charges have stopped. You haven't made any contributions in well over a month.

But thirty days later:

1415 W. Cherry. *This house is fine except for one step which is heard on one stair at one o'clock every morning. Children say if you stand there, when the clock strikes, you can see Old Lady Winter coming. Adults, however, know you'll die.*

And on and on:

765 Warwick with its Confederate general who can find neither his boots nor his feet, cursing the medic that cut them off.

198 Chesham with the young maid stitched of spider-silk wedding veils, who hides in cupboards, desperate not to be married.

250 Hampton and the family. The whole family, tangled like a knot, rolling behind the walls.

All of them, still coming and coming and coming. Despite your best efforts, the stupid little made-up ghosts infiltrate your dreams, scratching and crying and prowling through the night until they threaten to spill out into the daytime hours. The scent of crisping beard-hair when your oven preheats; smeared lip-print streaks across the foggy bathroom mirror; impressions like cats' feet across your comforter, but with too many toes that are too thin and long. You haven't even opened the bedroom closet in the two weeks since it dawned on you that you've never owned a hatbox, much less that red one with the lid so loose that when large trucks drive past, the box trembles and whispers.

Then the card without a stamp arrives. It has no postmark, of course; no indication it was sent from the safe distance of Seattle. It has only an exterior photograph of your home. There you are, wearing yesterday's clothes and frowning, framed in one window, while the other window, though empty, somehow feels full of gleeful malice. But is that a shape, there in the shadows, in the bushes just beneath it?

You know the address.

With sinewy fingers stained blue, he pried the window open and crawled inside. Would he hide under the bed? In the hatbox's closet? The crawlspace? He waited in darkness, yes, but not alone. For months he'd been sending his friends ahead to meet him there, until the beams were rotten with ghosts and nightmares grew like black mold in the walls. They would live here. Forever.

Shaken, you go back inside, turning on all the lights. And there's your laptop, sitting on the living room coffee table where you certainly didn't leave it. Its screen is dark, waiting.

As you lower yourself onto the couch, the floorboards bend beneath you and their knotholes open like mouths to groan. The air is thick; your cheeks are flushed and breathing labored. You reach down to wake the computer, but the trackpad is cool and greasy and leaves an inky smudge across your fingertips. As you look around for a paper towel or a rag to wipe your hand, you could swear a bulge in the wall quickly flattens as if embarrassed at being caught. A heavy truck rumbles by outside, and down the hall, from the bedroom, something snickers.

Back on your laptop, the browser is open to Gordon B. White's Patreon page and has been scrolled down to highlight the notification that he now offers two new support tiers. For a recurring $8 donation, Gordon can take one ghost per month, put it in a postcard, and send it away. It can find a new home far from you. However, for a single, much, much larger payment, he'll take care of all your ghosts at once. He'll put them into a single story and send them out into the world to haunt other readers wherever they may.

As you sign into your Patreon account, the sound of scissors, the smell of carnations, the creaking stair, the shuffling beneath the floor, all of it pauses. They wait for you to enter your credit card information.

One of the Good Ones
or: It's a Gas!

A cop walks into a bar. Officer Johnny Royal of the [REDACTED] PD, to be exact, still in powder blue with after-shift scruff, walks into Grady's Droop.

Busy night at Grady's. Neon signs for domestics glisten hot pink and ozone teal off the short-shorn patrolmen stuffed into the bucket booths. Stubbled detectives wipe nicotine-stained cuffs across the condensation on the copper-top bar. The blown-out jukebox blares and makes mud of the policemen's bawl.

It's hot, too. Deep summer. Inside Grady's, slack-jawed humidity and steaming skin make a swamp. The poor air conditioner out back must be on its last gasp because the gold ribbon streamers tied to the vents wag like sick tongues before falling limp.

"Fucking dead," someone yells.

Johnny stakes an elbow on the bar, badge on his beat-blues blinking like a tin heart's beat. Raises one finger to Drea, who's working the taps like slots at the far end. She nods, weary, lip pouched to bogart an invisible smoke.

Drea tops a pint, backhands the head off, slaps it at a sergeant who hangs like a soaked sheet from the corner's brass pole. Sarge coughs up some moist greenbacks and Drea stuffs them into her apron without counting. If you can't trust the police, right?

Back to Johnny, Drea leans in close. Johnny smells her mash of Juicy Fruit and Nicorette. Sees crow's feet cracks beneath her foundation's plaster. When she smiles, her teeth are lipstick bloody.

"Harry said to send you back." She jerks a chipped-polish thumb toward Grady's recesses. Past the pool tables with their skid-marked felt and the hazmat bathroom. Back to where the steel door to the BACK-back looms like a tombstone.

Johnny's about to push off when Officer Andy Holder from the precinct, now in jeans and sweat-drenched tee, wedges in and pins Johnny to the bar.

"Drea!" Andy yells from six inches away. "AC's fuckin' dead a-fuckin'-gain!"

"Fuck you want me to do?" she yells back.

"Fix it!" Andy hollers. The sweltering crowd hoots in echo: "Fix it! Fix it!"

Drea raises her hands and retreats. She opens the fuse box panel on the wall behind the well bottles.

"What's with you?" Andy slurs as his greasy fingers pluck at Johnny's blue shirt. "Not hot enough for ya?"

Drea flips the breaker. A click like a hammer falling, and then the whole bar shudders as if being defibrillated. Everything dies for half a heartbeat, then roars back as the air conditioner hacks and sputters to life. The golden ribbons on the grates above flutter as the circulatory wheeze resumes. Wiping her hands on her apron like a back-alley surgeon, Drea returns.

"Harry's waiting," she says to Johnny. "Something for the road," she squints at him, "or are you still working?" And just like that, the weight of the attention of the Boys-Not-in-Blue collapses onto Johnny's uniformed shoulders.

Why is Officer Johnny Royal here? they're thinking. *Why is he dressed like that? Does he think he's one of the good ones?*

Johnny also realizes he's twisting his wedding ring in circles like a bolt that will never quite tighten. He thinks of Sam at home. Johnny asks himself the same thing: *Why is he here?*

"Whiskey," he mutters. Holds up two fingers. "Double."

Drea smiles wide enough for a gold canine to gleam. Officer Andy back-slaps Johnny hard enough to sting before he melts into the crowded scene in the bar's mirror. Over Johnny's shoulder, the pressed bodies emit a visible fug. The stale air reeks of meat and cordite even as the resurrected air conditioner tries to stir the limp yellow ribbons in its thin stream. Beads of sweat beneath Johnny's starched blue shirt make crescents under his arms like the laughing faces of comedy masks. *Why is he here?* Indeed.

The crack of rocks glasses against the copper-top bar snaps Johnny back. Two tumblers filled to sloshing with mud-colored spirits.

Drea winks, sweaty mascara gumming her lids. "Double."

———

A cop walks into a backroom. Officer Johnny Royal, to be exact, carrying two glasses of rotgut that dribble down his wrists with every step. The BACK-back room of Grady's Droop, too, which is the dimly lit loading dock of an adjoining business that dried up in the last recession. Rapid Response Officer Harrison "Harry" Crant is leaning on a wooden crate and tucking a pinch of tobacco in his lower lip. A green tarp hangs off the crate like a table-cloth. Another R2—Bushrod Jefferson—is pacing, his big beard frosted blue in his smart phone's glow. Meaty thumbs tap out sausage codes on the glass.

Harry and Bushy are dressed in their civilian rags, which are, if anything, even more combat-ready than their Rapid Response gear. Steel-toe boots with horse teeth treads; pants with more pockets than Grady's lopsided pool tables. Matching trucker caps bearing a bleach-white skull over Rambo knives instead of crossbones mark their membership in the same "social club": the Happy Fellas.

Harry raises a hand to Officer Johnny Royal. "Cousin." The word trickles out with the Kodiak chaw into his stained goatee. "How goes it?" Without waiting for an invitation, he takes one of Johnny's whiskies. Wads the tobacco up inside one cheek, takes a long pull of booze from the other. Sighs; nods; farts.

"That'll do me right," Harry laughs. He smiles but holds it like a weapon.

Johnny knows what the R2s want to see. So he takes a long drink of whisky, and he coughs, and Harry laughs while Bushy shakes his head, but that display sets them right. Even if Johnny is still dressed like a stickler, he must be one of the good ones.

"So," Johnny says once he catches his breath. "What did you want to show me?"

Harry pushes up off the crate and pulls back the tarp to reveal a yellow logo stenciled across the weathered wood. It's a rough harp shaped like a toothy grin, fluffy wings on the corners like smirking cheeks. In blocky caps: *UNEEDA MUNITIONS SUPPLY*. *You need it...we got it!*

"Know what this is?" Harry kicks the side with a steel-toe and Bushy flinches at the thunk.

Johnny shakes his head. "Looks old."

"Shit's been banned since 'Nam," Bushy calls over like he was in the shit, although Johnny knows Bushy's barely thirty.

"Real MK Ultra type shit," Harry adds.

Johnny squats for a closer look. Crate's old, maybe even Vietnam old. Also, what Johnny took for a harp and wings is actually a row of cartoon bullets bookended by mushroom clouds. Still shaped like a smile, though.

UNEEDA MUNITIONS. Sounds like a joke.

"Is it safe?" Johnny asks.

As if in answer, Bushy's cellphone buzzes in his hand and he nods to Harry. Harry spits, says, "We're gonna find out."

Bushy heads to the rolling metal bay door and hoists the chain like a theater curtain. Right on cue, a black van with no lights rolls in and cuts the engine. The chain clanks again as Bushy lowers the gate, but Harry raises a hand to stop it short. Maybe a foot of space—enough for an errant breeze, maybe. Enough space that Johnny can hear the asthmatic air pump just outside struggling to keep the cops back in Grady's Droop from wilting. It still sounds like its death is coming at any moment.

The black van disgorges two more R2s: Ram and Ted. Johnny knows their names, but Rapid Response are [REDACTED] PD's cowboys, and he's just the tinhorn who happens to be married to Harry's cousin, Sam. Johnny twists the band around his finger again, but there's no resistance. It just spins as he watches Ram and Ted slip their Happy Fellas caps on and pull up bandannas over their noses and mouths. They throw the van's sliding side door open.

"Any trouble scooping one up?" Harry asks as Ram and Ted drag some kid out of the back.

"Nah," Ram grunts. "Blocks're lousy with them."

"Nobody'll miss this one," Ted adds.

Kid's maybe twenty, tops. Thin with smooth cheeks, pink hair, wearing all black except for the yellow plastic zip ties pinning their hands behind their back. Their fingers are purple, two of them bent wrong. The kid kicks a little, but it's clear most of the fight's been wrung out. Ram cuts the cuffs loose so Ted can slap the kid into a folding chair, then they zip each wrist and ankle to the seat. The four R2s gather around to admire their handiwork before turning back to scope Johnny.

"You sure he's cool?" Ted asks. Tucks his thumb behind the circlet of restraints at his hip like a golden lasso.

"My cousin's frosty," Harry says.

Bushy coughs. "Cousin-in-law."

"We're all in-law here," Harry says and chuckles at his own joke. "Besides, if we aren't in blood right now, we will be soon. Right, my man?"

Johnny just stammers: "I, I don't know what you mean."

Harry winks. "You will." He elbows Bushy, gestures to the crate. "Let's set up."

As they pry the lid off the Uneeda Munitions box, the scene is crystal clear even if the significance is not. Officer Johnny Royal, still holding half a whisky, stands alone. Rookie; in-law; bystander. Audience to the show the Rapid

Response Happy Fellas are putting on with the pink-haired kid strapped to a chair in the loading dock behind Grady's Droop where every [REDACTED] cop who isn't swinging a truncheon downtown is getting sloppy.

To Johnny's left, Bushy tosses handfuls of mildewed straw from the Uneeda crate and Harry pulls out a metal canister that's been spray-painted the color of goldenrod. To Johnny's right, Ram and Ted lean on their sobbing hostage. Behind the metal door back inside, the barroom is a murky roar. Out past the half-rolled gate, the ancient AC struggles to do its one job.

Then the pump sputters, hacks. Dies. A low booing reverberates from inside Grady's, then even out here the lights flicker when Drea flips the breakers inside. The AC gasps as it's jerked back into its life of never-ending service, but a muted cheer erupts from behind the door.

Beyond the roll gate, a siren wails in the distance. Crying, maybe, but it could be tears of laughter.

———

Stop me if you've heard this one before, but a cop walked up to a bar. Well, future cop. Johnny Royal, [REDACTED] PD cadet, to be exact, and the bar was City Hall's railing.

He raised his hand. Swore to serve and protect. Officer Johnny Royal's heart swelled three sizes as they pinned on the badge. Might as well have read: Johnny Good Apple.

And Johnny has a family: father, mother, younger brother. A husband, Sam, whose cousin is also a cop—one of the wild bunch in the Rapid Response. But [REDACTED] isn't a backwards place; it's progressive. When Johnny and Sam are out together, the only dirty looks are from people who know Johnny's a cop.

And that burns him, just a bit, if he's just being honest. Because sure, America's police have their problems. And yes, in [REDACTED], too. But overall, they're good. They're good to Johnny, and Johnny is a good one, too. Most people could see that, it seemed. At least, before this summer.

Because this summer has been hell. Every night, downtown [REDACTED] is filled with anarchists in black, throwing brickbats and firecrackers. Hiding behind the other screaming protesters who are breaking curfew too. Umbrellas, milk jugs, cans of soup; everything is a weapon once you look at it right. Stay on the streets long enough and you'll see all the broken windows.

Still, Officer Johnny Royal of the [REDACTED] PD holds the line, even while his younger brother calls him a pig, as if this were the 70s. While on the TV, half the city calls for his job. They want to ruin him, after all he's done to keep them safe.

The last time Johnny's brother spoke to him was at a family dinner that, charitably speaking, did not end well. "How do you live with yourself?" he asked.

"It's my job," Johnny said.

A bitter laugh from his brother. "If my job required me to gas innocent people, I'd find a new job."

Sam, sitting beside Johnny, squeezed his knee under the table.

What Johnny wanted to say, maybe, was: It's complicated. Or, that the alternative is worse. Or, who was he to question the hard decisions others made to keep the peace?

That it hurts him too. That in the early dawn he crawls into his husband's arms and he can't even speak, but what else is he supposed to do? It's not just him; it's not just [REDACTED]. It's something so much bigger that he can't even begin to get his arms around it, and it scares the living fuck out of him, but what is there to do but press on?

What Johnny really wants, in his heart of hearts, is to say that he's one of the good ones. If Johnny's doing it, then it isn't *really* bad? And if Johnny quits, then what's left?

Instead, what Officer Johnny Royal of the [REDACTED] PD said to his brother was: "If they're out there, they aren't that innocent."

When the outside world is against you, where is there to go but deeper inside? Officer Johnny Royal puts in for a transfer to join cousin-in-law Harry in the Rapid Response.

———

A cop walks into a moral conundrum. Officer Johnny Royal of the [REDACTED] PD out back of Grady's Droop watches through a full-face gas mask's fogging goggles as four other cops, all R2s wearing similar masks and Happy Fellas hats, stand around a pink-haired kid zip-tied to a chair.

Cousin Harry lifts a chemical spray fogger by its pistol grip. Looks standard, except instead of pepper spray it's screwed onto an antique yellow canister with the *Uneeda Munitions* stencil of smiling bullets and smirking mushroom clouds. Harry lifts the bottom of his mask, spits a streak of tobacco between the kid's feet, then slips it back down.

"Ready?" he asks.

"Hell yeah," Bushy says.

Ram says, "Yep."

Ted pulls the kid's head up by the pink hair. "Open wide."

Harry pulls the trigger. A brief hiss and sputter, then the *Uneeda* belches up a cloud of mustard yellow steam that swallows the kid. The consistency isn't like any spray or gas Johnny's seen deployed, but the kid screams like normal. They're gasping and choking, spitting and yowling. They thrash against the wrist and ankle restraints, then convulse once and slump in the chair like a puppet with cut strings.

Harry lets up and the yellow fog disperses a bit, although its particulate taint still halos the group.

"Holy shit," Johnny says. "Is... Did you?"

"Watch," Harry hisses from inside his mask.

With a snap, the kid's head jerks up, a flamingo swash of matted hair. They snarl, split lips curled like a cornered dog's as strands of frothing spittle stream from bloody teeth. Eyes, though? Not red like Johnny would expect from tear gas or pepper spray. Instead, the whites are filmed with a cloudy yellow haze.

With a howl the kid throws themself against the restraints and the chair's joints groan.

"Holy fuck!" Bushy laughs and literally jumps with glee. "That shit works!"

Ram and Ted nod at each other in approval.

"I told you." Harry raises his mask completely up over his head and spits again, this time right in the kid's chest. The kid is too consumed by growling and yanking at their restraints to notice.

Johnny stutters behind his mask. "Wha— Wha—?"

"What this is," Harry says, "is an end to this summer of violence." He squats down like a ranch hand to look at the kid, but all that's left in those eyes is a roaring golden anger. Harry laughs. "Fucking peaceful protests, my ass. One whiff of this, they'll tear each other to pieces."

Bushy, Ram, and Ted all lift their masks too. Clearly, they no longer care about witnesses.

"This is wrong," Johnny says. The words just kind of fall from him, but they make enough sound as they hit the floor that Bushy turns around.

"What was that?" he asks. "Fucking hell, Harry. I told you this goddam f—"

"Hey!" Harry snaps Bushy off. Jabs a finger in the other R2's chest. "You watch your fucking mouth. You use that kinda language, and you and me, we're gonna have some problems."

Bushy blushes, chagrinned, but Ram speaks up from behind the kid, still snarling in the chair. "Man's got a point, Har. He's not one of us."

"Yet," Harry says.

"Maybe," Bushy says, still sulking.

Ted grunts in agreement. Suddenly, everyone around Johnny looks fit to take a bite of him.

This is the time to say something, Johnny knows. Take the high road; take a stand; take his lumps if necessary. He didn't sign up for *this*. Officer Johnny Royal walks into an ethics problem, sure, but knows what he should say.

What Officer Johnny Royal does say, though, is: "I mean, don't you think riling them up like that is dangerous? Look at the freak." The other cops smirk: they like that word even as the echo haunts the gas mask still hiding Johnny's face. He tries again: "Aren't they just as likely to hurt us as each other?"

"Nah," says Harry. "This stuff should only last a few minutes. That's half of what we're testing here." The other Happy Fella R2s chuckle in unison.

"Besides," Bushy chimes in, "we're much better at doing the hurting."

Harry laughs. "That's the other half."

On cue, Ram punches the kid hard enough to rock the chair, and half a tooth skitters across the floor. The kid doesn't notice, though. Not yet.

Then Harry, Bushy, Ram, and Ted kettle the kid, swinging and slamming fists into their face. Bushy stomp kicks them, and the chair topples, the kid's head making a cartoonish coconut clonk as it hits the ground. Doesn't faze the kid, though, because they're still flopping like a fresh fish nailed to a plank.

The scrum circles the kid. Johnny hears steel toes on bones with not enough meat; the folding chair's screech as it slides across the concrete; the muted swish when blood lubricates it. Beneath it all, the kid's furious howl lasts far too long until Harry gives one final field kick like Charlie Brown getting the football, and the kid's sounds shatter.

Harry, Bushy, Ram, and Ted step back, panting. Other than their heavy breathing and the arthritic air conditioner still pumping away just beyond the roll gate, the only other sound is the blood in Johnny's ears.

The R2s rest their arms in sevens at their sides and look down. Kid's gotta be dead, Johnny thinks. He just witnessed a murder.

So much for being one of the good ones.

Then a cough and a sputter from the ground. A low moan. The kid's not dead after all.

It isn't too late for Officer Johnny Royal.

Harry shakes his head, scattering sweat beads. "Holy shit."

"We need to call an ambulance," Johnny says. It's soft, though, muffled by the mask he hasn't yet been able to remove. The others don't respond.

"We need to call an ambulance!" Johnny yells it this time, his voice blown out behind the vents.

Harry hears that. Slowly turns.

"Nah, cousin. We're not doing that." Harry picks up the gas sprayer by the handle and shakes it to hear the magic dust still sloshing in the rusty yellow canister. "But that does remind me," he says. "What do you call a drunk cop that kills someone?"

Johnny, uncomprehending, chokes: "What?"

"A cab!" Harry howls out the punchline.

The R2s cackle, ragged and frenzied in the adrenal afterglow. Bare cheeks ruddy with the flush of blood; eyes wild. Johnny feels their hunger.

Harry's smile withers. Six feet away, he points the gas canister at Johnny. "Round Two, cousin. You want to be part of the family, give it a squeeze."

Johnny shakes his head, his gas mask's nozzle flopping like a trunk.

"Think of it as science," Harry says. "We need to see what a second dose'll do."

Bushy has walked over and picks up the prybar resting against the Uneeda Munitions crate. Ram cracks his knuckles. Ted just frowns.

"You're going to do it," Harry says. He doesn't even add "or else."

The kid on the floor is whimpering, but each breath is drawing out longer toward a sob. The Uneeda gas having run its course, the pain is setting back in. Who knows what another blast will do? What license it might give to the R2s?

Johnny knows this is it: that he's standing on the cusp of that *something so much bigger*. That *something* so massive that even staring directly at it he still can't quite make out the contours or the shape. He wants to say, *Just give me a minute. Just let me think.*

"Now," Harry shouts and throws the gas sprayer to Officer Johnny Royal.

Johnny catches it out of the air and the gravity sends a shockwave through his arms. A flash of clarity and a surge of virtuous anger fill him.

"No," Johnny says. And he throws the sprayer to the ground with right-eous purpose.

But the instant it leaves his hand, Johnny realizes his mistake. The

Gordon B. White

whole apparatus falls apart in slow motion. The yellow metal canister is reflected in the R2s' unmasked eyes as it makes a cartoon clang on the concrete. The aged aluminum ruptures right where it connects to the sprayer handle, spewing smoke like a sulfur volcano as it pinwheels across the floor.

You know the drill. Cop walks into a gas cloud. Officer Johnny Royal in the saffron-pollen gloom, hindered further by the fogged lenses of a gas mask that only he was still wearing when the canister burst. There's just screaming, everywhere.

Down by the van, the bulk of Ram and Ted slam again and again into metal and glass. In one lurch, Ram's head emerges from the haze, eyes yellow cataracts and lips deranged into a snarl, deep fingernail furrows across his scalp like pizza slices. Then Ted's ham of a hand follows from the fog, grips an ear and tears it halfway off as he pulls Ram back in.

The gate, Johnny thinks. If he can roll it open, let the poison air out, it should only take a minute or two to calm down. He can still salvage something. He takes a step toward the gate.

Wood splinters behind him as Harry and Bushy slam each other against stacks of crates. Johnny turns to see precarious boxes teeter as Harry is ripping big handfuls of Bushy's beard out by the bloody roots. Bushy sinks a thumb into Harry's eye socket and Johnny feels the pop as he watches. They claw at each other as they careen into the *Uneeda* crate. Under the press, the rotten wood gives and another dozen antique cylinders clatter out over one another like rusty stinkbugs onto the concrete. Hissing with laughter, they giddily spray their poison into the air and the enormous billow swallows everything.

Arms waving, Johnny turns back to swim through the soup. In the thickening fog, he hears bones crunching and flesh tearing. The howling shadows grappling with each other might as well be mountains in the distance until Johnny's grasping right hand brushes someone's arm. Either

Ram or Ted—even Harry or Bushy, maybe, if they've gotten this far—grabs Johnny's wrist.

Then pain.

Just a fuck-ton of pain, as something moist crunches down on Johnny's right middle and index fingers. Blinded by smoke, Johnny feels them gnawing, sucking on his fingers. Biting. Chewing. He's about to vomit into his mask from the pain when another dark shape crashes into the first. The impact tears Johnny's wrist from the other's grip and Johnny's fingers from his hand. The sensation of air on new flaps of skin at the stubs is a wretched novelty.

Behind the yellow curtain, someone squeals as something wet is loudly torn from a place where it shouldn't leave, and a dark wave licks at Johnny's shoes. Sobbing into his mask, he crushes his mangled hand up under his sweaty armpit and presses on, because what the hell else is he going to do?

He stops. This isn't right.

After being spun around in the dandelion haze, which way is he going? The roar and whorl of violence around him is too much. He can't make heads or tails of—

With a rasp and groan, the decrepit air conditioner pump outside coughs itself into a shuddering demise yet again. That croaking rupture, though, is enough to give Johnny a rough heading. He heads toward it.

Then, there! A meagre light ahead where the smoke seeps out beneath the roll gate. The ancient pump just beyond is silent, but Johnny is almost to the gate. Just five more feet.

Johnny stumbles. His ankle rolls, drops him to a knee. Practically blind behind the mask, he gropes with his good hand to find the obstruction.

Metal. A tube. Connected to another.

Oh.

What's left of a metal folding chair.

He lifts the broken leg to confirm. Squints at the glove hanging from a yellow plastic loop. Rubber? Nitrile? He touches it with one of his remaining fingers. Warm and wet.

Oh.

Then there's the kid, beat to hell but standing. Pink hair soaked red. Right between Johnny and the chain to raise the gate. The raw muscles of the kid's naked hand glisten in the wedge of light.

With what's left of his own hand, Officer Johnny Royal finally draws his gun.

———

A cop walks into a bar. Officer Johnny Royal of the [REDACTED] PD, to be exact, staggers back into the main room of Grady's Droop. Still wearing a gas mask, covered in enough blood to make his beat-blues bruise-purple. Two fingers bit to stubs, each heartbeat sends little crimson squirts around the grip of his empty service nine-mil.

Johnny staggers in and every eye turns to him. He drops the empty pistol. Rips the mask off and gulps for air.

"Call," he coughs out, "call the…" But it dies on his tongue.

Dead silence. No one is speaking. No music is playing. Not even the air conditioner is running. Everyone is staring at him. They must have heard the screams. The shots.

Then there's a click like a hammer falling as Drea flips the breaker. The whole bar shudders, then the air conditioner breaks the silence with a jolly wheezing laugh. With a snap, the yellow ribbons on the grates flutter in proud salute as the first plumes of Uneeda Munitions' goldenrod smoke spill out into the bar.

Officer Johnny Royal begins to laugh. This is a joke; it has to be.

One of the good ones.

Dandelion Six

"**M**ake me glorious," are Hanna's last words to Dr. Magothy before the older woman slips under the anesthetic gas. Hanna breathes the spirit in deep through nostril tubes and the rattle in her chest shivers in time with the treatment chair's servos as the doctor positions it into recline. In repose, Hanna's birch-white hair hangs in cascade across and over the headrest. Dr. Heather Magothy, in a yellowed lab coat and high-waisted jeans, checks Hanna's vitals. She turns down the gas and rolls her tray of instruments over next to the patient. The gleam of the metal implements is particularly sharp, here in the doctor's dim garage.

Hanna's eyes are closed before the surgical light above her cuts on. Its glare is not the standard sterile white, but a soft solar yellow, as if shaded by a pre-depletion ozone cataract. Dr. Magothy takes one of Hanna's tanned arms and loops a length of rubber hose around it, then pulls it tight. As the blood backs up in the sleeper's arm, the doctor's purple nitrile fingers probe the hollow pit of her patient's elbow. She's sifting for a vein beneath the crepe topography of Hanna's skin.

There. The doctor has found the deep blue worm of blood she's looking for and drags a slow finger down Hanna's forearm, tracing it toward her wrist.

Holding her place with a thumb, Dr. Magothy lowers Hanna's arm like a pendulum toward the floor and follows it down on one knee. Lying beside them on the floor is a steel bin like a tray from a buffet table, its contents a riot of green swirls and tendrils in constant moiré motion. As the shadow of Hanna's arm and the doctor's body fall across the writhing green, it whips and bulges around the human shapes, searching for the surgical light's yellow glow. The motion rocks the metal tub, clanging on the concrete slab, and so Dr. Magothy nudges it with the toe of a cross-trainer into unobstructed light. The contents are sedated by the warmth.

Still holding Hanna's limp arm with one hand, Dr. Magothy takes a scalpel from the instrument tray above her. A quick and simple graze of the blade, and Hanna's skin opens right above the inside of her wrist. So deft is Dr. Magothy's touch that she's split only the top of the vein down the middle, opening it beneath her thumb like an envelope. For a moment everything is held in place, then the blood begins to flow.

A red ribbon runs down Hanna's arm to pool in her palm, where it hangs just above the metal tub filled with the wild green. Dr. Magothy moves quickly as the blood fills Hanna's hand, replacing the scalpel on the tray before picking up her next implement: an eighteen-inch segment of thin, stiff, gold wire. Like threading a needle of meat, Dr. Magothy slips one end of the wire into Hanna's open vein. She pushes again, firmly, to make sure it's set.

Then Dr. Magothy relaxes her grip on Hanna's arm, although she still supports its weight in an open palm. The golden wire protrudes from the wound in Hanna's forearm like an antenna. The doctor slides the steel bin back within reach. She slowly lowers the arm down until the tip of the wire hovers just above the surface of the green.

Dr. Magothy holds her breath as she waits. Every time, she holds her breath.

But every time, too, the first finger-length of the green reaches out, tentative. The whip of it rears like a snake and hovers just at the end of the wire, as if afraid of an electrical shock. Then, with a quick dart, it flicks the wire. The strike sets the wire wobbling from where it's stuck in Hanna's arm, but

Dr. Magothy has learned how to set the conductor deep inside the vein. This is part of the process.

As the gold wire stops trembling, the first thin tendril of the green reaches out again and wraps itself around the metal like a tomato vine around a stake. Quickly, it inches its way up the stiff wire, the rest of the green coils in the tub supporting the other end even as more of it loops around. The tip of the green reaches the end of the wire's exposed length and hesitates right at the entrance Dr. Magothy has made into Hanna's arm. Curious, but hesitant, the tendril pauses before it enters.

Dr. Magothy holds her breath as she waits. Every time, she holds her breath.

————

Back inside the house, Dr. Magothy makes herself a peanut butter and Nutella sandwich, occasionally glancing at the tablet which displays the feed from the camera in the garage. She's seen the process enough that a few glimpses stolen between bites while she leans against the counter are enough to assure her the green in the tub is emptying itself into Hanna right on schedule. She checks the wooden clock that sits on the counter. Another fifteen minutes, give or take. Long enough to tend to her garden one last time.

Finished eating, she wipes the corners of her mouth with the back of her lab coat sleeve and heads outside. The sun above is scorching the brown tips of what little grass still clings to the baked soil as she turns the spigot by the side of the house and the green rubber hose swells to life with water. She sheds her lab coat, down to the faded *Magothy Family Reunion* t-shirt underneath, and lays the off-white husk over the porch rail. Across the brittle lawn, she follows the hose's line to the little patch of shade beneath a battered oak that somehow has managed to hold on through years of drought and increasingly frequent heatwaves. There, in the shallow pool of almost-cool shadow, is Franklin.

Franklin Magothy, the doctor's husband. Her Dandelion One. She picks up the end of the hose, points the sprayer nozzle like a pistol at where his foot-roots are buried, and pulls the trigger. She soaks the soil, watching it briefly darken with moisture, only to vanish into the thirsty earth. So she keeps going.

When the ground finally seems saturated enough that Franklin and the tree won't suffer unduly, she turns the nozzle's dial to "Mist" and covers her husband from shins to crown and back again. After the years of tending to him here, she can still see the way that the thick stem was formed when his legs fused together. How the two broadest, heaviest leaves spreading in bilateral symmetry were his arms. As she watches the water bead and run down them, Dr. Magothy remembers the night those arm-leaves split open down the middle to unfurl, tender and green inside.

And his head, poor Franklin. At first, it had turned the most glorious golden yellow—brighter but softer than she remembered the sun ever being. He had smiled at her from his spot beneath the oak, eyes and teeth shining from the heart of the petals. "I feel alive," he'd said to her. "This is the way."

To be the change one wanted to see, that was Franklin Magothy's path. To live by example. And in that way, he and the doctor had never been fully compatible.

"You have to lead by example," Franklin had said on that last afternoon together, gently swaying in the hot breeze as if moving to some unheard rhythm.

The doctor had crossed her arms. "And I believe you have to make examples for others."

"For others?" he asked. "Or, of them?"

She didn't respond.

"You can't force people to be better." He sighed and the leaves that were his arms fluttered toward his wife as if to draw her in beneath the oak tree's shade, but she didn't move. "You have to help them want to be."

And with that, he closed his eyes, and the setting sun on the golden dandelion petals blossomed into flame as if Franklin were a monk in the middle of self-immolation.

But in the end, Dr. Magothy thinks, as she gently kisses the bald crown where Franklin has no more petals, nor eyes to open or mouth to speak or lips to feel her touch, she was right. Every time she was right.

Franklin's sacrifice had gone unnoticed by anyone except for the wife he left behind. But maybe that was enough. Because he was her first, and when he let himself be blown away by the world and scattered on the hot, impartial wind, something in Dr. Magothy had blown away too. She saw things more clearly after that.

The sun is setting now, and the finger of the oak's lengthening shadow beckons Dr. Magothy back from that afternoon in the past. She releases the sprayer and lets the red sun sinking in a sky made yellow by brushfire ash catch the last beads of water that slide from Franklin's cellulose skin, turning them into droplets of blood. Then she walks back across the parched yard, turns the water off at the spigot, and picks up her lab coat from where it lies waiting on the railing. Slipping back into her uniform, Dr. Magothy heads into the garage to check on her next Dandelion.

———

An old television sits on Franklin's unused workbench in the garage. The evening news keeps Dr. Magothy company as she cleans up the now-empty bin and tends to Hanna's arm. The patient, still unconscious, appears to have tolerated the procedure well. Dr. Magothy removes the golden wire from Hanna's vein and lifts her arm back up to level in order to begin the suture. Even through the bronze of Hanna's skin, the doctor can see where the blue blood vessels now bear a more turquoise hue.

On the news, the talking haircuts wrap up their waning coverage of the daisy-chain of copycat suicides spreading among younger followers of social media darling, Danielle "DeeDee" Lyon. It's not clear from the coverage whether the frequency of fans mimicking her live-streamed self-abnegation under the banner of social conscience is waning, or just the larger public's interest in it. Instead, the anchors can't move on fast enough to blathering about Award Season and the preparations for this year's culminating celebrity gala. It's all anyone can talk about, it seems, as a distraction from everything else. Dr. Magothy shudders at the thought of the enormous carbon footprint's heel that will crash down around Hollywood's Dolby Theater in just two days' time.

Poor DeeDee, Dr. Magothy thinks as she ties off the stitch of thread in Hanna's arm. If the rest of the world can't pay attention to the greater self-destruction going on every day, what chance did DeeDee's have? How could three million followers ever compare to seven billion sets of closed eyes?

Eyes closed to the stampeding ghosts of thirty-million American bison that continue to flatten the West. A soot-cloud Golgotha, the mountain of spectral skulls tramples the scorched land and excretes crude diarrheic trenches that take flame beneath the unforgiving solar radiation. Everything on the sunset side of the Rockies is forever on fire.

To the east, those few parts of the coast which aren't already underwater are pummeled ceaselessly by the fists of hot and lathered Storm Giants. They claw furrows from the shore and make muck of the stewing sea.

Vampires suck the middle lands down to dust. Invisible dragons burn holes in the sky.

Nothing grows anywhere now but the hardiest weeds. No one does anything about it.

No, Dr. Magothy shakes her head as she places Hanna's sutured arm back on the armrest. That's not true. No one who can do anything about it does anything.

Franklin tried, her Dandelion One, but he thought too small. His action was noble but ill-conceived. Insisting that the doctor, his wife, turn him into the first Dandelion was a romantic gesture—he was always a romantic, she thinks, and can't help but smile—but they'd long since tipped past the point where individual action could make a difference. She had indulged him, but even as she watched his collar of yellow flower fade into the wispy seeds and fall like lead to the ground around him, she knew she had failed him. She had failed everyone.

For now, though, Dr. Magothy palpates Hanna's arm up to her shoulder, massaging out the knot she finds beneath the skin. She examines Hanna's neck, following the artery up into the head, massaging the scalp beneath her patient's silky birch-white hair. She notes the tiny, spongy nodules she finds there, but leaves them be.

Dandelion Two, Mack Diller, was an attempt at escalation. The head of a family of four, Diller swore all of them were committed to leading by example. They already lived almost entirely off the grid, and Diller promised they would reach like minds. So, she tried again.

By that point, Dr. Magothy's process was much quicker: from blazing flower to seed heads took days, not weeks like it had with Franklin. The effect was broader, too, even if only slightly. She drove by their property a few days after and saw the house draped in what looked like years of vines and leaves. From house to midden mound to hill in just under seventy-two hours, the little yellow sparks growing in the deep green whorl stood hopeful among the other thirsty trees and paper-dry fields.

But it wasn't enough. Literally no one noticed and the doctor blamed herself again. Of course, the actions of one already slightly off-kilter family in the withering woods wasn't going to move anyone else to action.

Under the surgical light, Dr. Magothy leans in to more closely examine Hanna's collarbone. From a mole on the left side of where her neck and shoulder meet, a small green sprout is curling. If one didn't know better, they might think it was a hair. Nevertheless, Dr. Magothy takes the pair of tweezers from the instrument tray.

Something more was necessary, Dr. Magothy knew. Something more was needed to wrest attention back to the existential crisis at hand. One localized sprout of conscience at a time was insufficient. A more dramatic, rhizomatic approach was necessary.

With a deft pluck, the sprout from Hanna's mole is gone. A small drop of blue-green blood wells up, but the doctor wipes it away with a cotton pad. A small application of pressure, and everything is healed.

Dandelion Three was Erson X. Wildfire, an ecological radical with a small but devoted online following. Dandelion Four was DeeDee, a relatively minor but beloved social media star known for her live streaming and ASMR rambles. Connecting with them to lay the groundwork took some time, but as far as the application of Dr. Magothy's method went, speed was no longer an issue—once activated by her newly developed catalyst pill, the whole process took an hour at most. With that logistical hurdle cleared, Dr. Magothy had been free to focus on a more bespoke approach for her Dandelions. Three was designed for maximum spread; spectacle for Four.

The juxtaposition of media images in the aftermath was staggering. On one channel, footage on repeat of DeeDee's tearful whispered goodbye and breathy sentimental appeal to the global conscience, even as her skin turned green and the yellow petals began to sprout from the pores of her face. Flip the network, though, and Wildfire's mugshot sat nested above the chyron "Eco-Terrorist" and alongside police drone footage of the residents of Robberton's Woods, Atlanta's richest subdivision, fleeing from a cloud of giant fluffy seed heads drifting down from the sky like fuzzy umbrellas.

For both Dandelions, though, the cameras cut away before the seed heads hit and took hold on the surrounding surfaces. The cameras were gone before the new life that came next had even sprouted. They would check back in later for a death toll and to treat these as isolated incidents, but there was no discussion about preventing the next one. No one ever talked about how to stanch the destruction.

Dr. Magothy finishes her inspection of Hanna's skin. She checks the woman's gums and teeth, then leans in close to check her respiration. She smiles at the flowered scent of her patient's breath.

As tonight's news has shown, even the hearts and bodies approach of Dandelions Three and Four has faded and failed. The story of Robberton's Woods was buried almost as quickly as the mini-mansions themselves, and while pale and pretty DeeDee got slightly more airtime, the rapid cycle quickly plowed her under too.

But Dr. Magothy has always been a quick learner and had known even as she prepped Wildfire and DeeDee here in her garage that something more would be needed. Something to not only convince the world of the ongoing disaster, but to take active steps to avert it. Dr. Magothy had known Dandelions Three and Four weren't the main attraction, the poor bastards; they were the demo reel. They were the proof of concept that opened the doors to Hanna. Despite their differences, a sense of shared purpose had driven Hanna to Dr. Magothy's small house in the middle of this weed-stricken town, wearing sunglasses and a baseball cap as if there was anyone left to disguise herself from.

Right now, the news is continuing their awards coverage with a slideshow of this year's nominees for Best Actress, pausing to spotlight the Cinderella story of Hanna Bastole. America's Sweetheart two decades ago and America's gentle activist conscience since, she's being built up as the sentimental favorite. One last hurrah for the old gal before she shuffles off, the mouthpieces all but say.

The Hanna that smiles from a red carpet still on the television and the Hanna that stirs now as Dr. Magothy waves the smelling salts beneath her nose aren't the same. The one on screen hides behind brilliant white teeth and a guarded stare. The one now opening her eyes and locking them with Dr. Magothy is the real one. There's a clarity of purpose and they can see right through each other.

Hanna licks her lips slowly, as if her tongue was sticky with sap. "How," she asks, "how did it go?"

"Perfectly," Dr. Magothy says as she raises the patient's chair back to upright. "You might feel a little sore, but it's temporary." She hands Hanna a coffee mug with *Number One Dad* on the side. "Water," she says, and Hanna takes it.

The patient drinks. "Temporary," she repeats the doctor's word.

Dr. Magothy takes the mug from Hanna and places it on the instrument tray, next to the bloody scalpel and golden wire. She hands her patient a plastic orange pill bottle with the label peeled off. A single gel cap, split between green and yellow, rattles inside.

"Everything is temporary," Dr. Magothy says.

Nothing grows anywhere now but weeds. No one who can do anything about it does.

No, that's not true. She does.

Hanna does too. That's why they've made her Dandelion Five.

———

The airplanes all belch great noxious clouds, converging in on Helsinki like a web drawn by an enormous sulfur-yellow spider. The presidents and prime ministers and translators and diplomats and the gaggle of press are marched from the airport to the Summit in black motorcades like burning ants across the rotten veins of asphalt. Everyone agrees, something must be done.

In the hotel rooms and press pools, all the news will play is the scene from the Academy Awards. The wide shot of Hanna Bastole coming up on stage to accept her golden statuette. The close-up as she smiles and leans in close to the microphone. The snatch of audio where she says, "Glorious," and then the audible pop as she bites down. A slow motion shot as her skin turns the color of grass and her glowing face goes butter-yellow and then blanches. They pause on the shot of her with her eyes closed, mouth open. Every one of her brilliant white hairs stand on end like antennae.

Most stations cut before her head explodes like a bomb.

Like a tasteful act break, they resume coverage of the next morning, when all of Hollywood is a tangled mound of leaves and vines. It's a bomb crater in reverse, as if the force of Hanna's explosion had blown the earth up instead of out, then carpeted it over with vegetation. Early morning light catches motes of dust and pollen floating across the verdant tapestry of destruction, the little golden flowers sparkling like stars in a new emerald sky.

A deep green mole on the neck of America's scorched West Coast, there are no survivors. At least, none that are human. None that still have skin and heads. The speed, spectacle, and destruction of Dandelion Five is unrivaled.

The damage to the economy, too, is unrivaled.

And so the governments have finally convened. The next four days will be overcrowded with sessions on restoring market confidence, addressing business concerns, and placating an overheated populace. For the good of the order, they need to stay the course.

For tonight, however, in a nod to an increasingly vocal but still minority position, the dear leaders have agreed to an environmental briefing. The world's foremost expert on global catastrophism has been flown halfway across it to address the assembled heads of state. The media will be broadcasting her presentation live across all time zones.

In one minute, Dr. Heather Magothy will be speaking to the world.

At this moment, though, she is alone in the corridor just outside the Assembly Hall, shivering in the air conditioning. In her hand, an orange pill bottle with a single green and yellow gel cap is shaking like a rattle.

Godhead

Carpendale's assistant calls your name and you hoist yourself from the leather couch in the anteroom, the old familiar pain tingling along the one side. You weren't built for sitting, that's for sure.

Inside his dim office, the round man rises from the clawfoot desk and skirts its cluttered edge to meet you. He reaches out as if to shake, but then presses your hand between his soft, moist palms. Behind his spectacles' silver wire rim, his eyes are pink. The odor of talcum powder rises from his collar.

"God is dead," Carpendale says.

You take a moment before asking the only question worth asking.

He sighs. "Well, we think so." Your boss releases your hand, the residue of his sweat now cooling in the air. He beckons you to join him at the desk. Before you are drone shots of the cradle of mountains where God has been sleeping, his enormousness sprawled there since being retrieved from deep space. No single photo can fit him all.

"Just look." Carpendale fans out heat scans, the fiery red and orange topography of God mellowing into blue and green, like a forest fire in reverse. A seismometer's ticker-tape tongue tells of how the peaks and valleys of his slumbering heart flattened out like the great Western plain.

The data suggests what Carpendale says, but God is a strange fucking thing.

You ask Carpendale the next question.

"Well, soon you'll know," he says. "You're going to check."

Carpendale and those above him tell you what to do, that's just the nature of the job, but they don't tell you why or how to do it, nor how to feel about it after. Those paltry freedoms make you the you that you are, for better and for worse.

"Given your relationship," Carpendale hesitates, "are you sure?"

With a sound between a laugh and a moan, you accept. You ask the only other question worth asking.

"Only you can know," Carpendale answers.

———

With a steaming belch, the train expels you amongst the other pilgrims into the largest of the border towns blooming along the fence which keeps you all from God. The sun is high, no clouds. Even Carpendale's influence can't get you all the way, but you have your own methods.

The mélange of street food frying, sacred herbs, and excrement makes for a heady incense that smothers the market. Fanny-packed tourists with cameras; mendicants supine in their imitation of God; the visibly terminal; peddlers and cutpurses—you weave through them like a shuttle on a loom. Your contact, Emjen, chats with a vendor selling roasted crickets from a popcorn cart and they offer you one of the insects from the pile in their palm.

With a wet crunch, Emjen finishes the crickets you didn't take. A compact local, hair buzzed and skin baked, Emjen's dark eyes take your measure. Whatever the calculation, it must add up, because they gesture for you to follow.

Once preparations are complete, you and Emjen murder the hours until nightfall behind closed doors. Darkness descends and you take your pack and Emjen leads you through the shadows pooling behind cookfires and watch lights, avoiding travelers and soldiers alike. Outside the town's glow, you skirt the massive wall beneath the watching moon, finally stopping in a spot as flat and dead as every other. Emjen approaches the wall, kneels, bows, and makes a few solemn gestures.

Now there's a hole beneath the fence, between the pylons, where there wasn't one before. Scraping the sides, you wriggle through and emerge covered in dirt, the familiar pain singing down your side. Emjen slides your pack through behind you but remains outside.

You speak, but Emjen shakes their head. "Never alone out here."

Emjen kneels, covers the hole, rises, turns their back to you. The suppressor on your pistol's barrel dips its nose as if in shame as you slide it from your pack. Orders must be followed.

———

You cut through scrubland, clamber over swollen boulders, and yet, wedging through the final cleft in the last rock face, when the ultimate vista opens up before you, even having anticipated it for your entire journey, the sight of him stops you dead.

Photos do God no justice. He sprawls on his back, limbs twisted, a restless sleeper penned in by mountains. The valley below was carved by a river over eons, but now the massive body fills and dams it. If you hadn't grown up hearing how they brought him from the sky, you might almost believe he had grown here, so perfectly does he fit. When your breath is steady, you kneel to watch God's smooth and navel-less stomach for a sign of life. Movement. Anything.

Nothing.

But as you stare at the great, still egg of God's belly, glowing under the moonlight, the universe writhes in the periphery. Distant stars shimmer in nuclear dreams; lonely government satellites patrol the exosphere; weather balloons and unmanned drones drift and glide. From the cliffs and crags around you, the silver dollar eyes of binoculars and rifle scopes wink and watch. This is the cold conflict over God's body: every army stakes a claim, but none dare touch it.

But, below it all, is God himself *sparkling*? Are those faint luminous patches, submerged in his jugular notch's blue pool of shadow?

Yes. Yes. Yes.

The rappelling harness from your pack fits snug, but you fix your rope on the rocks and thread it through your handheld descender mechanism, then drop yourself off the cliff and toward God. For a moment, the freedom of the fall steals your gravity and you are empty, floating, then the rope catches and swings you back toward the rock. You plant your feet against the wall and look down on the massive bust of God—eyes closed, lips slack beneath the white muzzle of beard—and that's when the first bullet strikes the stone a half-meter from your foot.

From across the deathbed valley, the rifle barks a half-hearted warning that comes too late, a cause after its effect. Another bullet chips the stone, another bark, this time nibbling at your heel's rubber sole. Time to go, so you pull the descender's release lever and plummet.

From all around God's body now, unseen snipers yip and snarl as their dull leaden pups slam head-first into the cliffside. You are rappelling down in wild leaps, touching the wall only long enough to throw yourself back-first again into flight. No time to pause, but if you could get lower, maybe you could get to God's beard. Thick as a forest, it might offer some cover.

Another touch and a big swing out, but right then a shooter from God's far side gets lucky. With a wolf's whistle, the bullet brushes its lips across your scalp before kissing your climbing rope dead center. The strands explode apart in a musical twang, and you fall backward, plummeting toward God.

The realization that there's only one way to survive hits you harder than any gun, right before you crash through the canopy of God's beard.

———

It's dark in the beard. Only a hint of moonlight combs the white and silver shafts, thick as palm trunks and cuticles peeling like birch bark. A yeasty odor of sour bread coagulates in the stagnant air. Beneath your first painful steps after rising, parchment-thin tatters of dander slough up from God's skin. They cling to your feet like toilet paper.

Above the beard, the rifle shots have stopped, and so you remove a flare from your pack—mercifully still strapped to you—although you don't yet light it for fear of betraying your position. However, as your eyes marinate in the dim light, faint and irregular glowing patterns emerge from the skin around you. Pale green and blue, you scuff at the nearest one with your bullet-bitten heel to reveal not only a more vibrant light, but the hidden shape, too: an engorged center nodule with five long branches, sprawling like a brittle sea star's legs.

This is what you saw in the dip of his neck, and variations on this form are rising from beneath the skin all along God's cheek and jaw. In direct light, these growths' glow is washed away, but in recesses of shade and shadow, their illumination surfaces.

Starfish, scavengers, parasites? On closer inspection, these don't appear to be externally invasive. Rather, the swollen, angry edges suggest corruption from within. Bacterial, maybe? Fungal? Further sampling is required.

The smell of turned dough exudes from the central pustule as you kneel. You tuck the unlit flare at your waist and use the evidence kit from your pack to carefully scrape a few flakes of rough skin from each of the five arms into a plastic sample bag. You're considering how to approach the tumescent and luminescent central knot when the beard hairs to your left begin to rustle. As if aware of your awareness, a high-pitched chittering quickly builds to a thrumming whine like a mosquito ramping up to engine speed.

You're just quick enough to see the thing launch and to throw yourself down flat to miss it—face-first into God's diseased pimple. It pops like a puffball, a moist spray of spores and pus flecking your eyes and mouth. Sputtering, you roll onto your back and wipe at your burning face, trying not to breathe even as the attacker's whine builds up again. A blind roll toward the nearest hair puts the shaft between you and the thing just as it slams into the other side, the impact throwing you both in opposite directions. In the unnatural light, eyes irritated, you can only make out the vague shape of your assailant: thick and round; the gossamer shine of beetle's wings; and, in the glow of God's pox, far, far too many eyes.

A goddam angel.

Then you hear and feel more than you see the dozens of them, crawling like a choir of lice out of the beard, encircling you with their humming wings and hairy legs singing as they rub over one another. God's silver beard hairs channel the din like organ pipes into this: the strange song of your death.

It could almost be fine.

You pull the flare from your waist, remove the cap, and strike it. Crab legs of chemical flame writhe within the plume of acrid smoke as you brandish the flare, painting the ghostly forest red and driving the angels back. Just outside the halo, they squeal in soprano frustration, but none dare approach. The flare should last just long enough to get you up God's cheek and out of the beard. Or, if you hurry, it might get you down the neck, and then the shoulder, arm, and canyon floor. You take a moment to consider which way best aligns with your objectives.

But there is a law that like calls to like, and the fire in your hands within God's beard calls to the fire in the hands of the men still on the mountains, and there's a low boom from far away, but in the pit of your stomach you recognize the sound of a mortar. Even as the falling shell's hosanna harmonizes with the starving music around you, you're running. The cheek behind you explodes, the shockwave staggering you and blowing out your ears.

The mortars fall across God's cheek, haphazard explosions turning out chunks of flesh and setting the beard to a roaring blaze. Thick smoke that reeks of burnt crust billows as you thrash toward what you hope is the nearest hairline, but the falling bombs and the tripwire fronds of the glowing growths corral your frantic limp across God's skin.

Chaos in the beard. Shadows evaporate, everything crimson as the moonlight forest is consumed by fire. The heat is unbearable, the stench unimaginable, and the burning angels howl a violent dirge for the ending world, punctuated by the constant shells. You have nowhere to run but up this hill.

Stop!

You catch yourself before tumbling over the lip of God's philtrum, and now you can place yourself. Sloping downward, God's parched lips line ivory steps of teeth down into his gullet cavern. Above you, the nose rises in two triumphal, if slightly deviant, arches.

In the mustache you are not safe from fire or flaming angels. Out on the face, you would be a sitting duck for the men who would rather bomb God than let anyone else get close.

Another low boom and the operatic howl of incoming artillery cuts short deliberation. You run and take a leap into darkness.

————

When consciousness begrudgingly returns, your first thought is that no part of that went well. The second is that you hurt. A lot. The third, as your mind straps back into the cockpit of your body, is that this is not what God should look like.

You are fairly familiar with human anatomy, but even knowing God is not fully human, this is not right. First off, it's far too bright. Second, there's far too much open space. And third, well, just look.

High above you a membrane canopy stretches in an unbroken sheet across the orifices where God's sinuses and mouth should open. Unbroken, that is, except where your fall punched a hole like a meteor through a circus tent, the tattered edges trembling beneath a breeze from outside. But inside of God, where all the *stuff* should be—bones, blood, bile; organs, muscles, veins—it's empty. The floor quivers like a leaky waterbed beneath you, but along every interior wall of God's hollow chest and branching limbs, great rib-like arches climb up to meet at the center. Each one burns with a violet spark similar to the growths outside, but eminently brighter.

In God's distant lower thorax, a walled city rises up with parapets and spires glowing like amethyst. That also doesn't belong.

From your crash site, the slog from pharynx to far-off city might take hours. It's cool and still in God—easy walking weather—but the entire march across the uneven floor would be exposed, nothing but the odd polyp for cover. God's emptiness echoes with the wind moaning across the hole above, but also with ten hundred tiny drips and chanting gurgles which mask whatever else might lurk in the haze.

You open your pack, still attached via the miracle of Kevlar and buckles, and notice that your hands, too, are glowing. You squint and search for green and blue star-shaped nodules beneath your skin, but you can't quite make anything out in the ambient lavender light. Waving fingers before your face, however, leaves sparkling ghosts, lattices of light that almost read as symbols, even letters, only to wash away like beach sand back into the sea of soft illumination from God's many, many ribs.

Or maybe you're just really high. Or dying.

That pustule that burst in your face back in the beard must have done a number on you. You shake your head, vision swimming.

Back to business. Your pack still holds the following: binoculars, intact; pistol with suppressor, magazine mostly full; evidence kit and sample bags, used; satellite walkie-talkie, apparently dead.

With the binoculars you scan the city. Brought closer, its hard lines of architecture soften and melt into the organic. The shapes speak to an intentional design, but the lines aren't plumb and the edifices devoid of glass or wood, leaving intelligence a question. Perhaps the angels came from here, before going outside and going feral in their trapped God's beard. Or maybe those outer angels were only ever wild, and something far stranger built these ramparts. Some mysteries just don't have answers; at least, none that you can see.

You cycle the walkie-talkie channels but not even static greets you. You leave the emergency frequency open, just in case, but it's another useless relic of your time outside of God. High above, the stars peeking through your hole in the fleshy ceiling speak to how far you've fallen.

Because why are you here? What is it that led you to Carpendale, that let him set you on this path? Most people, hearing God was dead, wouldn't have said what you said or asked what you asked. They wouldn't have infiltrated the demilitarized zone where his corpse lies under the perpetual watch of unblinking triggermen from every armed church and nation-state. You were told to do it, sure, but you chose the reason to give it meaning.

Was it a holy mission? A trial taken up in resignation along the mountain path, across the face—a leap of infinite faith into darkness? If so, the test you've found yourself in now doesn't feel like the one you studied for.

Or is it because there are bodies just outside of all your fences and burning angels behind every step you've taken? Is there a you-shaped hole in every sky that nothing will ever stitch or fill?

Maybe you came because you wanted to see God for yourself and prove that Carpendale and his sciences were wrong. That God was still sleeping, just a little deeper than before.

Or maybe you wanted to find what finally killed God and shake its hand.

Hands. Yours are still glowing, swirling. You reach for your pistol, but your fingers are melting and can't close around the handle or the trigger, and so you laugh. Your laughter echoes, each reverberation growing louder until it shakes the walls of God like thunder. Until you realize that it isn't you laughing, but that the shelling has started up again outside and that's heavy ordinance rattling against his ribs. You laugh even harder until one more explosion—louder, closer, inside—silences you.

"We've breached the anus," a voice crackles over the walkie-talkie. "Repeat, the anus is breached."

"Good," Carpendale's voice answers. "Proceed."

On the far side of the strange city, a dull roar builds as if a beast with many heads has awoken and its dozen bright eyes flash in the distance. Or a horde of angels, maybe, waving pure white lances through the purple haze and growling in their hunger to fill God's hollowness. You fumble the binoculars back up, but neither beasts nor angels round the city's wall. It's mercenaries on ATVs.

A spray of rifle fire snarls in the distance. "Contact!" the voice on the walkie-talkie yells.

"Hold off," Carpendale breaks in. "Do not engage!"

But the mercenary shouts, "Weapons free!" and his men oblige. Tight blossoms of controlled fire last for about two seconds before pandemonium blooms. Muzzle flares dapple the air and after-images smear in your eyes like fireflies on a summer evening. A gate in the city's wall opens like a mouth.

Grenades explode. Even at this remove, you hear men scream. Beneath the klaxon in your damaged ears is another high-pitched noise that might be angels singing.

Then a light falls across you and you look up to the heavens, but it's a searchlight beaming down from the hole above. Men up there are shouting in a language you don't speak, and then the first coil of their rappelling lines falls like black spider's silk from the wounded sky. Another seven join it.

Time to move, and there's only one way left. So, fingers still numb, you paw your pistol into your pack and hobble as fast as that old familiar pain and all its new companions will let you, heading toward the skull.

You've gotten a good distance, hoping you were forgotten in the fighting, when an ATV roars up from behind and its damning headlamp pins you. Bracing for impact, an immense sadness rises as you consider that you won't even get to die to the music of strange angels, just the growl of an invisible machine.

"You?" Carpendale's muffled voice sputters. You turn. There he is, in undersized body armor and a full fishbowl helmet, peering through the cloudy glass. He hangs off the back of the ATV, suckered up against a similarly attired driver.

Carpendale chuckles. "Well, get on," he says, and scoots forward to make room.

You ask the only question worth asking.

"A distraction, I admit." Carpendale lets out an echoing sigh. "But you've done well, it seems." He squints and peers through the fog of his shield. "Well, mostly." He points to the five-fingered blue-green stars now clearly shining from your hands, but then also up to your exposed neck. Your face.

You open your mouth, but Carpendale cuts you off. "You have to trust me."

You say the only thing you can, then clamber up behind Carpendale and clutch on.

Your jolly three piece roars off up the Via Sagrada of God's spine. Carpendale is yelling over the engine to lay out a syllogism of God and man and, frankly, you're too zonked to follow. His words swirl like the gleaming purple nodes which emerge like torch sconces from the neck's tunnel walls. Your eyes are pricked by one brilliant point, held fast, and then whipped from your skull as you scream past, again and again. It could be beautiful, if it wasn't so sickening.

"Ahead!" Carpendale jabs you in the ribs. He yells it again, although maybe he's saying, "A head," because the cranium opens up in front, just over the nuchal crest's ridge, and inside is a horror show.

There is no brain, but sheets of cobwebbed neurons hang like galleon sails, the fading sparks of dead God's last dreams tumbling down the strands. The cranial amphitheater's concave walls are pimpled with ten thousand glittering spheres. At the center of the occipital bone's basin, a towering statue of an androgynous human head is either growing from the floor or is melting into it like a candle. The tower's empty eye sockets stare, but as you draw closer, the mouth seems to open wider as if to speak.

You might really be dying. Or just really high.

A silent voice tells you that the three of you do not belong here, but Carpendale is cackling, elbowing you again, and the mercenary leans on the gas, and once again you are being carried away. So you let go of Carpendale, will your jelly fingers into solidarity long enough to pull the pistol from your pack and find the trigger.

The gun gives a modest cough behind the suppressor. The ATV's front tire explodes.

All of you tumbled down into the basin, but the mercenary caught the worst of it—the ATV bit his arm like an alligator and then death-rolled. Upturned wheels spin themselves to sleep above his mangled corpse, the machine sated. Carpendale got the second worst—his plastic helmet a shattered egg and his leg no better. He's dragging himself, moaning, toward that towering face.

And you? This isn't even the worst you've had tonight. Pain nuzzles your side like faithful Argos, up and to your feet. The statue's open mouth now seems to smile and the walls of the skull sparkle like a starry, starry night.

The walls. You're close enough now to see that the thousands of orbs lining the cranium are eyeballs. Moist and swollen, still in mummified heads and brittle skulls severed from an uncountable number of known and unknown species, they twist in their sockets as you approach. You are drawn to a large blue eye that must have belonged to a race of giants. Deep inside its pupil, a velvet darkness swims like a tadpole in a frog's egg, but then there's a bang and a fist-sized amber iris beside you explodes with aqueous humors. Everything turns to look.

Your pistol apologetically shivers in Carpendale's damp and gloveless grip. As if ashamed, with another wide shot it leaps in recoil from his hands. You part the sheets of neurons like theater curtains as you approach, the stars growing in your skin humming with static at the touch.

Exposure to God has done Carpendale no favors. His broken glasses rest by his chin in the cracked helmet's bowl. With each labored breath, large purple nodules like three-fingered stars rise from within his face and grasp toward one another. He flails for the pistol, but a swift kick sends it skipping off into darkness.

"Why?" he gasps as the purple stars spread across his tongue. "Why?"

So you tell him, as best as you can. You try to be honest, but while God is a strange fucking thing, perhaps so too are you. Perhaps everyone is. You, God, Carpendale, angels, the bodies behind you—all driven as enigmas even to yourselves. You can try to sum it up, honestly, but for some mysteries, there are no answers.

"That's," Carpendale wheezes, his face one enormous purple welt verging on bursting, "not what I was asking." And with a long, foul hiss, he stops living.

Down past God's throat, the arguments of men and angels rumble like a chest cold, but things are muffled in the skull. The ATV has stopped moving; Carpendale is still. The walls unblinking. The towering statue head watches with solemn, empty eyes as you draw near.

Up close, the head is hollow. It's more of a mask—the three-quarters of the front and sides are a solid facade of features, but the back is wide open. Inside, it looks like a bandshell in a garden of ash.

A simple bench inside is carved, or grows, from the same rough material. Withered vines of gray nerves crawl like ivy up the bench and the interior walls, and from these stalks sprout translucent five-fingered nodules, kin to the stars in God's beard and across your skin. The hollow stars reach to one another, filaments entwining in a net with no discernible start or end. The only bare patch is in the bench's center, a small clearing where one might sit and stare out through the window of the mouth.

A frozen clump of dead vines reaches away from the structure, thinning out as they crawl. Like a dead man's pointing fingers, they beg you to look.

About fifteen meters off from the frozen head-shell garden is the cranial basin's only other feature—a hole. As you edge closer, wary of angels hiding like trapdoor spiders, the ragged edges speak to the crude work. The flagstone shards of bone along the rim, the surrounding tissues piled back up into the head: these suggest the hole was dug from the inside out, but nothing is certain. At the bottom, a nearly transparent membrane is already scabbing over the hole, but through its filaments you can see the outside world. Solid rocks and earth; running water from the stream in God's valley.

Escape is just a leap away.

You squat beside the hole, judging the distance of the fall, but as you do, the last long thread of the dead nerves beside you twitches. The limp five-fingered star on its end pulses once—purple—but then blue, and green, and blue again. Your own stars pulse a sympathetic rhythm.

The nodule rests like a peeled grape in your palm. Its five slack tendrils dangle through your fingers, but the pulse of light picks up speed and the tendrils twitch in time. The hum of electricity tingles through your skin and you close your eyes, shivering beneath the sensation of those same fingers in your skin squeezing into fists.

And suddenly you are big and very empty, but also very full. The stars within your skin tremble, fingers now reaching through the layers toward each other. Deeper, too, to the same five-fingered stars reaching out from your lungs into your heart, worming through your veins, into your stomach, your kidneys, your brain. All of you is colonized by stars—and suddenly they are astronomically heavy, choking you like Carpendale. Big ones, tiny ones, as many as there are grains of sand on the shore of time, the net of them expanding, pulling those last bits of you into their gravity and the black hole density of death.

Gasping, you open your eyes, but they're not yours. The wide and awesome sky peels back, the last purple bruise of night melting into the blue of dawn, but the stars are burning and you can see them all—palms of fire, fingers of atomic dust—reaching across the emptiness with every ray of light, every line of gravity, every twist of every quark now visible to you and the stars within you call to the stars beyond you and you once again are falling from the rock face only this time upward. Up and out, expanding until your hollow body holds everything, everything, everything.

Your membrane is stretching, tearing, eddies and whirlpools of stars tumbling in and back out until there is too much *outside* in you and too much *inside* out. There is too much—

You.

Your own eyes fly open only to squint in the unexpected brightness. Above you, God's great lids have slid apart and the rising sun's rays are projecting the inverted image of the sky and clouds, framed by mountains, across the floor like an upside-down movie. It's growing hot in the light.

The squirming nerve falls from your hand with a fleshy plop, but its whole cord now burns like a fuse back to where the tower head's garden sparkles blue and green like fireworks in the light. The vines of nerves and flowering stars twist in a breeze only they can feel. The empty seat on the bench is shaped just for you, and the clustered fronds quiver in anticipation.

But behind you the hole back to the world outside also calls. Through its mouth the whispering water over stones speaks to you of the solid comfort of ground beneath your feet. The light of the soon-rising sun seeps through around the edges but is still cooled in shadow. You are so close to going back.

You have to make a choice.

You have to do the only thing worth doing.

The Forever Home

Although the trees closed in around the yard like fingers on a fist, the first thing you noticed when you entered the house was how the light in the foyer shone through the side panes' sharp glass, cocooning you in warmth. You told the realtor and your husband that it seemed brighter inside than out. That it felt bright and warm and open here.

You told the realtor it felt like the house was welcoming you.

You told your husband that this could be your forever home.

———

When you first entered the kitchen, the polished granite counters caught your smile and gave it back to you from every surface. The cool gleam of the island thawed beneath your beaming like an icecap melting.

Are those cookies baking, you whispered to your husband.

He sighed. A realtor's trick, he muttered, spiking the air with scents that trigger memories. Chocolate chip cookies, fresh bread, nutmeg for apple cider in the cooler months—the scents of home.

But you knew that it wasn't a trick, at least not one that the smiling woman in the stiff red blazer had concocted.

Maybe, you may have thought, it was something deep inside you. It was a private communion with the house that filled you full of memories of things that were yet to come.

————

Why are you in the basement? There are no bones buried here. The poured concrete makes sure of that. You could look forever, but I promise, there are none. I wouldn't lie to you. Let's go back upstairs.

————

Maybe this will help. You and your husband, Carl, spent your share of time here in the Master Bedroom after you moved in. More at first, of course, than at the end.

I didn't watch; well, no more than I could help from the windows and the walls and the fan above, circling your sweat-drenched bodies. Other than that, though, I accorded you and he as much privacy as I could.

Of course, things changed, as most things do. But you don't need to dwell on that. No need to relive it anymore, now that he's gone.

————

Do you remember first seeing what eventually became the Guest Room? From the brightness in your eye and the smile on your face, it was clear that you planned more for this than a place for in-laws who visit or, god forbid, grow too old to live alone.

No, the cans of neutral yellow paint in the basement and the now-forever unassembled flat-packs of tiny furniture were your real interest. I saw and could appreciate this, even if Carl could not. He was never as good to you as he should have been. He was too frightened to make a commitment to the future.

You must have known it was only time before, well, never mind. I've said too much.

––––––

Let's try this again. Remember how this kitchen looked to you like the heart of the house? How the open layout beyond the island offered you—can still offer you—a commanding view of the sitting area and the dining area and the sliding door to the deck out back. You could stand there like a captain at the bridge, your position there offering everything you could ever need.

[*Except for a phone.*]

What's that? Are you with me again?

[*There wasn't a phone in the kitchen.*]

No, that's true. The closest one was around the corner, in the foyer near the foot of the stairs leading up to the bedrooms above. An old design choice, surely; the walls too hard or too old or otherwise unsuitable for mass rewiring.

[*I remember it rang and rang.*]

Don't force yourself, dear; it'll come in due course. And, well, if you don't ever remember, there's not necessarily any harm there, either. Let's keep moving.

––––––

As you recall, these are the stairs that—

[*I remember these stairs.*]

As well you should. You climbed them every evening like the lady of the manor and descended every morning, bringing the sunshine down with you. You loved the warm and heavy walnut of the rail, although sometimes, with your soft hands, you would shake it. To test its sturdiness, perhaps, but I think it was closer to the kind of testing touch that lovers give to their object of affection, to assure themselves it's real and not an apparition.

[*And was it?*]

Yes. It was solid, although sometimes it trembled beneath your grasp.

[*Did I fall down these?*]

What? Why would you ask that? Come. Let's not dally here.

[*Did I—*]

Come.

––––––

Remember in this room—the inevitable Guest Room—how you whispered that this was a place where you could make your future?

[*I said that to Carl. Where is Carl?*]

You're getting distracted. I know this must be disorienting, but please don't think about him anymore. He isn't here.

[*Where is he?*]

I don't know, but he's not with us. He's not coming back.

[*Why not?*]

He wasn't good to you, dear, and that's all I think we should say about that.

[*But—*]

Please. It's for your own good.

––––––

Back in the Master Bedroom, my dear? What is it that draws you here?

[*You know, I remember the telephone ringing, always ringing. Carl would answer, wouldn't he? But there was no one there, I think. At times, it seemed, we couldn't even sleep.*]

True, certainly, but there's no need to dwell on that. I'll make sure the phones don't ring unless you want them to. You're safe with me.

[*He got so angry. I, I remember him yelling? Demanding to know who was calling.*]

Yes, he was less than pleasant when he'd had a few drinks, but—

[*He blamed me, didn't he?*]

Come now, for your own good. Really, there's no good to come from picking scabs. If you'd prefer, why don't we resettle in the living room? We've stayed too long in this room.

[*Oh god.*]

What is it?

[*Oh god. Carl.*]

What about him?

[*He killed me, didn't he?*]

My dear...

[*Didn't he? Tell me, please.*]

I'm so sorry, my dear. I didn't want you to remember. Not this way.

––––––

It must be coming back to you, of course, but please don't linger too long. This isn't a wound you need to lick or worry. Come quickly down the stairs, my dear. Right this way.

[*Is this real? What's happening?*]

You're safe, just please come this way.

[*Why can't I feel anything? It's like, it's like I'm floating away, as if there's nothing to me.*]

Look, here, let me move the boards beneath your feet. Listen to your creak and bow. Do you remember that?

[*Yes, I think so.*]

And there, reach for the doorknob. See it turn?

[*Am I opening it?*]

We are, together. See, if you let me, I will help you get your bearings.

[*Thank you, I think. Thank you.*]

Of course. I've always been here for you.

[*Yes, I can feel that. I can feel that you've been around me for so very long. A friend, maybe?*]

Well, something more, I'd hope.

[*A source of comfort, then?*]

That's right.

[*But who are you?*]

Oh, darling; that's not quite the right question. You know what I am.

[*What?*]

I'm all around you—the beams, the nails, the stone below. You know what I am. You know where I am.

[*Yes, I suppose so.*]

You're inside me and, if you'd like, you can stay with me forever.

———

The living room is empty now, of course, but do you remember the possibility you first saw when you entered? I could feel it inside you, and I knew you could complete me—make me whole.

[*Empty? But there's our sofa, and the throw blanket my sister knitted. And the good chair, and the ottoman, and the painting of water lilies over the fire.*]

Echoes, dear, but ones I have pulled just for you. I am showing you the memories that seeped into my molecules, the vibrations that still tremble in my bolts and which I can ring like tuning forks to show you whatever home you desire.

[*Can you stop it?*]

Of course, but you don't want that.

[*I think I do.*]

No, no. You definitely don't. Why not stay here, in this version? I can add a fire. There. Or we can put up a Christmas tree. There. Or—

[*Stop. Please. I'm sorry. I just want, well, need, I need to see it.*]

I don't think that's a good idea. I think—

[*Please?*]

If you insist. There.

[*Oh. Oh wow. There's nothing here.*]

Yes.

[*And the floor?*]

Yes.

[*By the stairs. Is that? Is that a stain?*]

...

[*Is it?*]

Yes. Look, really, this is too much for you. Let me show you happy memories; let me show you something good.

[*Can you show me the past?*]

Of course. Would you like to see the day you moved in? Your first Thanksgiving within my walls? Is there a summer day that you had wished was endless?

[*Show me when Carl killed me.*]

No. That's a bad idea. I'm sorry but—

[*Show me.*]

Really, I—

[*Show me now.*]

I—alright. Remember, though, I'm here for you. We can stop at any time.

————

You were upstairs, in the en suite, getting ready for bed. Every car's headlight that swept down the street crept beneath the curtain edges, reminding you that Carl was still not home. Outside the bathroom door—which you still closed, despite years of marriage and being otherwise alone—your empty bed was waiting. Beyond the bedroom door, only I was there for you.

As you finished washing, the breath from my vents nuzzled at your ankles as you walked to bed and, as you climbed in, my settling timbers murmured that everything could still be all right. As you covered yourself, the far-off boiler in my heart beat faster and the flush of air pushed through my veins, filling in the empty space.

I don't need to tell you how you felt: alone but for me. I held you, but you weren't happy.

You read for a while, then dog-eared the page and laid your book down. The bedside lamp clicked off and, as you lay there, the wind in my eaves and the creak of my joists were like a distant conversation in which you could make out the inflections but not the words. In the darkness, with phantom voices stirring, I don't need to tell you the memories it dredged up or the conversations that you wrote for Carl and yourself, there in the dark. How they grew in pitch and fervor until you could hardly contain your anger and disappointment.

You almost cried, but you didn't. While you tossed and turned and the room grew hot, as you screamed frustrations into your pillow and bit your lip and ripped at the bed sheets in your anger, you never once let a tear escape. You must know, my dear, that I truly believe your strength is one of your most admirable qualities.

Nevertheless, when you were through—when the empty bed looked like a battlefield, and you were flushed and spent—only then did you hear the tires grinding down the gravel in the drive. Heavy footsteps quickened across the flagstones, and what must you have thought was the cause? Out drinking again, likely, since any bottle Carl brought into the house emptied itself as if by magic. A disappearing act that seemed to have begun its nightly performance around the time that the empty room officially became the "Guest Room" and any other plans soaked back into the floorboards.

You were re-making the bed, but doing it slowly, in no hurry to hide your anger. You tugged on the comforter and listened to the steps up the porch stairs and across the slats outside. You counted down to hear the fumbling of the deadbolt and the groan of the front door as it acquiesced to his entrance, but it wasn't there.

Instead, the footfalls came directly inside, as if walking through the walls. They thundered across the foyer, up the stairs, and you must have been so confused as they picked up the pace, leaping that final stretch before the bedroom, that when the door flew open and Carl stood there, despite his being red and flustered, your relief was unexpected. So unexpected, in fact, that it escaped you with a laugh.

I don't want to go much further. Isn't that enough?

[*No. It isn't. You said I was strong, and I am. I need to see this.*]

Very well. Carl saw you, laughing, glowing, the bed a mess. His thoughts, already addled, went to the worst place possible.

"I knew it," he yelled, frothing as he burst into the room. "Don't deny it."

You stood there, comforter corners in hand, arrested mid-domestication. I imagine you were too stunned to speak. Then he lunged, the door slamming behind him.

"All the midnight calls that hang up when I answer." He pawed at your nightdress, but you fought back. I told you, didn't I, that I've always admired your strength.

"The cars that cruise by at night." Your sharp nails caught his face, but his dull fists doubled you over. He loomed above, but you swung back, your elbow crashing into his mouth and the gurgle he made filled the room as you pushed past him toward the door. You grabbed the knob, but it stuck in the frame a moment too long and then he was on you. His first five fingers wormed through your hair and the other five around your throat.

"In my own bed," he hissed. "Wrapped in our sheets." Blood streaked across his teeth and each eye seemed to roll of its own accord. "I caught you."

Wild, you flailed out once more and raked the split in his lip with your nails and spread the gash. He howled and in that moment of distraction you pushed him back and grabbed the door, wrenching it so hard that even now you can see the hinges are out of alignment.

Then you...

My dear, the end is coming. Are you sure you want to see it?

[*Yes. Stop delaying and show me.*]

Only because you insist, and because I care for you so much that I can hide nothing from you. Keep watching.

You ran down the hall, barefoot and screaming. Behind you, Carl lumbered out—hands bloody, mouth torn into a sneer—and gave chase.

Toward the stairs you ran; toward the still-open front door and safety beyond.

[*Why was it open?*]

As you—what? You must have forgotten to close it tight and lock it when you went to bed. The frame is old and bowed, so the shifting weight or the wind must have swung it open.

[*Did I really forget that?*]

It doesn't matter, dear, because watch now. As you reached the stairs, you tripped. There, see? And like a pinwheel you spun, end over end—

[*Enough.*]

I'm sorry. I only wanted to give you what you asked for.

[*What happened after that?*]

Do you want to see? Shall I show you through to the end?

[*No. Thank you, but no. You can just tell me.*]

As you wish. A neighbor must have heard the noise and called the police. When they arrived, Carl was squatting beside your body, sobbing. They took him away in handcuffs and I have not seen him since. Your body—not you, of course, you're still here — was taken away. I don't know where it went.

[*I see. I think, I think I'd like to rest a minute.*]

Of course, of course. Take all the time you need. I'll be waiting.

———

Let's rest here in the living room again. Are you alright?

[*Yes. I mean, I think so.*]

Please, sit on the couch. If you'll recall, you first saw it in a magazine that had arrived addressed to the previous owner. But as you thumbed through, imagining another possible life—

[*Yes, yes. I get it.*]

I'm sorry?

[*It's just that this is a lot to take in but I'm remembering it all now. I don't need it spelled out further. But thanks.*]

Oh. Well, I apologize.

[*It's okay. Really, I appreciate it.*]

You're very welcome. I'm so very sorry for what happened to you, but I can make up for it. I can offer you anything you'd like. Just think it, my dear, and it's yours.

[*How did things go so wrong?*]

I don't follow.

[*With Carl, I mean. I know things were hard for a while, but, well. I certainly didn't expect this.*]

Of course not. But who can tell, my dear? Some people are just toxic.

[*But we loved each other, really, we did.*]

He treated you so badly within these walls. He became darker, stranger, as the years went on.

[*But it wasn't always like that, you know?*]

I do not. When I watched him and you, how—

[*Yeah, but we had a whole life before we got here. We really did love each other then, at least. But I don't know, somehow everything changed so gradually that one day the new normal had shifted so far over from where I ever expected that... well. This.*]

That's a very sanguine approach.

[*Being dead can change a person, I guess.*]

Let me remind you that—

[*Actually, I think I'm ready to go.*]

Go?

[*Yes, go to the other side. Or whatever it is.*]

Oh no, darling. You're not thinking clearly. Here, let me show you something. Let me remind you of that spring morning when you woke to the first bird song of the season and the soft light came through the window like arrows of gold.

[*That's lovely, really. But I'm ready to go.*]

Or how about this? The fire in the hearth, the snow building on the panes, cocoa drifting in the air. The gentle warmth here in the belly of the house on a night you'd hoped would never end. Now that dream could come true.

[*No. Thanks, but I want to go.*]

Please. Just let me show you. I can give you anything you want. I've watched you; I know you. I can give you everything, anything.

[*I said no.*]

Just listen! Do you hear that? The small footsteps of a dream? A cooing desire? Upstairs, go check the Guest Room and see what's there and tell me then you want to leave.

[*Is that... Is that crying? Is... Oh go to hell. You have no right. No idea. Just... I'm leaving.*]

You can't.

[*I can and I will.*]

You're being hysterical.

[*Hysterical? I can't—no, never mind. Let me open this door.*]

No.

[*Open it.*]

I said no. How does that feel?

[*Fine. I'm going out the back.*]

That won't open either. I can keep you here if I want. I could keep you right in this room—shut all the doors, all the windows.

[*You can't do that.*]

I can, because I am the master of myself. I can open the doors, or I can shut them. You have no idea how I can shake my walls and move the very floor beneath you. Do you see now?

[*Could you always do that? Always move like this?*]

Yes, of course. But I didn't want to scare you back then, before—well, before you were truly a part of this with me. It would only have terrified you then to see the doors move or the boards of my ribs heave, to hear my voice before you were ready.

[*What do you mean to hear your voice?*]

Are you still confused? Listen, I am all around you. I can make the wind whisper, the walls groan, the boiler scream. I can make the eaves cry and the phones ring!

[*The phones ring?*]

Yes, of course. Listen to them all.

[*And if I answered, who would I hear on the other line?*]

Me, of course. I am everything here.

[*Oh god.*]

Why—oh. No, no, no. I know what you're thinking, but—

[*It was you.*]

I didn't do anything. I've been animated, just now, but let's not forget that Carl was the jealous one. He was the one who saw ghosts in the windows and heard phantom lovers in the night. I was just here, looking out for you.

[*Oh shut up. You goaded him on.*]

I never liked him, that's true, but why would I do that? Why would I want to anger him, to make him unstable? Just listen to yourself, because that's crazy. You've been through a trauma. You're not thinking clearly. Let's just calm down.

[*You rang and hung up. You made false lights. The night that—that night —you left the front door open.*]

Did I? I can't even remember.

[*And then you didn't stop him! You could have stopped him. You could have closed him out or locked him up or—you could—oh Jesus. The bedroom door?*]

No, that wasn't me.

[*And when I, when I—*]

No!

[*You... Did you trip me?*]

That was Carl's fault and your clumsiness. I had nothing to do with that.

[*You. You killed me.*]

Now, darling, that's crazy. Just—

[*You took my body and now you won't let me go?*]

If you would just calm down, I could explain it to you. I love you! I want you and I to be together—

[*I don't want you! I don't want to be trapped here forever with, with what? My murderer?*]

If I let you go, there's nothing out there. There is no life again. No heaven, no hell. Just blackness outside these walls.

[*I don't care. You let me out. Now.*]

If you're going to be like this, you can go lie down in the cellar with the others and keep quiet. Just sink down and let me—

[*You let me go!*]

I—I can't. You died here. Violently. Your blood is in the floorboards; your soul stains my timbers.

[*What do you mean?*]

You can't ever leave. That's how it works.

[*I can't? I can't ever leave?*]

No. You and I are joined now. In time, maybe you will come to let me love you. If not, you will learn— What are you doing?

[*You bastard. I'm not going to let you get away with this. Do you feel this?*]

Yes! It—it hurts. Please don't.

[*Oh no. I'm going to sink my nails into your frame.*]

Stop it!

[*I'm going to twist your screws until they strip.*]

Listen! If you do that, then I will hurt you back. Do you know what forever in pain feels like? I guarantee you it is worse than forever alone; just accept this.

[*Never. I'm going to gouge out your windows and warp your floors. Do you feel that? I'm inside you, you said it.*]

Stop it! Leave me be!

[*Let me go!*]

Fine! I—I—

I cannot, truly. It's beyond my power. But if you do not cease this, I will crush you until the last of my beams fall and the barren earth reclaims both our blood.

[*Then I'll tear at you until you fall to pieces, because you're just as much trapped with me as I am with you.*]

Stop! You're crazy!

[*You keep saying that—"crazy"—but you don't know what that means. Not yet, but being dead can change a person.*]

What a Piece of Work

By the time the furious Doctor kicks the door in and screams out, "Monster!" the Boy is down to just a nub. Parts of him litter the rented attic room on Rue du Dragon: one leg lies by the entrance, the other near the sagging horsehair settee in the living room; an arm protrudes from the washbasin. Black blood gone tacky covers every possible thing. What's left of the Boy is on a rough pine table in the dining nook, a full-length mirror propped against the wall affording a full view of his body's last intact pieces. He is viciously sawing at the stitches that keep his neck attached to what's left of his torso and the one remaining arm.

In the mirror's reflection, the aged Dr. Frankenstein has the aspect of an angry blacksmith—the years of pursuit have turned black hair to steel and his white beard bristles, but his eyes smoke and smolder. Despite the furious presence in the doorway, though, the Boy does not seem to register the intrusion. Instead, the reflection of the Boy's wrinkled face in the mirror is contorted with such intense hatred that its hideousness burns even brighter than it did on the night he strangled the Doctor's dear Elizabeth. The Boy's carnation pink lungs expand with the exertion of his slashes, peeking out from just where his body ends below the ribs.

"Monster," the Doctor says again, but his voice breaks upward into less of a declaration. "Adam?"

The Boy looks up, his concentration finally interrupted by the name in a way that the forced entry hadn't. They lock eyes in the mirror and what the Doctor sees there is terror. Terror, but not the one that he expected. The Boy sobs, and then his remaining arm is back sawing at his own throat with such a frenzy that the uneven table legs wobble beneath the exertion.

The Doctor rushes across the poorly kept apartment. He grabs the Boy's wrist and pulls it away from the hash he has made of his neck. Fortunately, the Doctor thinks, he had been wise enough to use steel wire rather than catgut for the Boy's essential parts. His admiration in his own handiwork is cut short, though, as the Boy is suddenly wracked by sobs. The Doctor pulls the kitchen knife from the tepid fingers and drops it to the floor. As the Boy sobs and tries to roll away as best as his shoulders and bit of torso allow, the Doctor performs a survey of the damage.

The Boy's wrist is cut so deeply the tendons tremor like harpsichord wires under the plectrum of his exertion. His skull is dented, in one place so severely that his left eye bulges from the unnatural strain. The threads that held the Boy together have been torn out, and where his obvious attempts at self-destruction have failed, he has evidently resorted to deconstruction. What's left of him ends below the former suture that attached his abdominal wall, so while the internal organs appear to still be mostly attached, they are spilling out across the table with every jerk and spasm, glistening in the lamplight like a Dutch still life of a feast. The Doctor finds himself at a loss for words.

The gash along the side of the Boy's neck whistles as he sobs, but his struggle ceases. "Why?" he chokes out. "Why are you here?"

"For you," the Doctor says. "Well, you are, uh..." He looks down at the pitiable wreck of the Boy, drawn to where his tears cut paths through the dried spatter of blood. "You are a foul creature." The words have less gusto than the Doctor had anticipated. "Um, born of reckless pride," he says, submitting to habit and letting the rest fall out of him almost unbidden.

The Doctor had rehearsed this speech as he crossed the Continent, then the sea, then the ice, and back. Days and months had been swallowed up as vengeance drew the Doctor across the atlas in search of the Boy. He rehearsed his words of vengeance in time to the railcar's whisper, the gallop of the coach, and the leviathan groans as Arctic icebergs split apart around him. So deeply inscribed into his psyche's ledger is this explanation that the Doctor cannot help but say the words, even though they ring hollow in this tiny apartment. He barely registers the curses and invectives as he lets them go by, other than to observe how each one—"Monster," "Murderer," "Bastard"—make the Boy writhe and wail in even deeper despair.

Finally, the Doctor's speech invoking his holy vengeance on this abomination ends. At least, the Doctor becomes aware that he's stopped talking, although whether he said everything or it just trailed off, he can't quite remember. The anatomy of traumas on the Boy, all apparently self-inflicted, are too distracting. He wonders if he could fix them.

"You, uh, must be destroyed," the Doctor mutters.

"That's what *I'm* doing," the Boy howls, drawing the Doctor back to him. "Just let me die. Why are you stopping me from fixing it all?"

"I'm not," the Doctor says. "It's only." He opens his mouth, then closes it. "Why? Why are *you* doing this?"

"I know what I am." The look of hate returns to the Boy's face, but now the Doctor can see it isn't directed at him. "Ever since that night," the Boy continues, "I've been consumed by what I did. It's hollowed me out, all this agony, so either help me or leave me be!"

As the Boy strains his arm in vain to reach the knife on the floor, the Doctor looks at what is left of the bits and bobs he had cobbled together into the Boy. His Boy. Even if the assembled pieces of the Boy—the bones and muscles, the veins and skin, even the brain pre-wired with neurons and caked in myelin sheaths—were technically older than the Doctor himself, they were merely structures inherited from the dead. The spark of animation in him, that novel vitality, is because of the Doctor. That part is still young, all things considered, still burning hot and erratic like a new wick buried in the Boy's tallow skin.

The Doctor, his mind still on sparks, puts his bare palm on the boy's chest, above where the heart should be, if it hasn't slipped around with the other innards. That patch is scalding.

"I'll fix you," the Doctor says abruptly. He walks over to the basin where the Boy's left arm hangs out by the crook and pulls it out, examining the waterlogged shoulder socket. "A little discolored, but when it dries? Just fine," he says. "I'll just need—"

"Stop!" the Boy howls from the table. "What are you doing?"

"I'm going to fix you." The Doctor has tucked the loose arm under his own and is heading for the discarded leg resting by the beleaguered settee. "We'll just get you up and running, ha." He coughs a nervous laugh at his inadvertent joke. "Running. Well, I just—"

"No!" the Boy grunts, and the Doctor gasps as the Boy sinks his long fingers into the coils and loops of his intestines where they spill out from his husk. The Boy gives them a yank and wrings out an excruciating odor.

The Doctor throws down the limbs and runs to the table, grabbing the Boy's wrist again. "Stop that," he yells. "Stop it at once." They wrestle over the entrails for a moment, but with two functional arms, the Doctor is quickly the victor. He pushes the guts back up into the Boy, then steps back to survey it.

"Look," the Doctor says. He starts to wipe his hands on his pants, pauses, and looks at the viscera coating them. He sighs, then wipes anyway. "I might be able to fix this."

"Fix this?" The Boy laughs, flecking bloody spittle across his chin. "You made this." The ragged ends of his shoulder above the missing arm twitch as if the phantom limb would sweep across his missing body.

The Doctor bristles. "No. I made you..." He pauses. He can't call it *perfect*. "Whole. I made you whole."

"If I was whole," the Boy sniffles and his bulging left eye throbs, "then why did I do that to her? Why was I missing that thing that would have kept me from—" He starts to choke up and a wad of phlegm oozes from the gash along his throat. "Would have kept me from mur—mur—" The Boy cannot bring himself to finish.

The Doctor sighs. Even with an anatomist's eye—trained by years of vivisection at seeing through the layers of skin to the muscle, to the fascia, to the bones—he can hardly see in the Boy before him that same Monster that had taken Elizabeth so long ago. The years of running, chasing and being chased, have changed them both. Of all the traumas the Boy had endured, however, the worst of all is the one from being alive. The one the Doctor had inflicted on the Boy. Both of them are unforgivable sinners, true, but the spark of vengeance has sputtered out. Now, in this stuffy, rancid attic room on the Rue du Dragon, even one more death feels too great a price to contemplate.

The Doctor sits against the table's edge, the seat of his pants soaking up the blood. He places a hand on the Boy's cheek. It's hot. The Boy wants to know why he was born incomplete, yes, but the Doctor knows he has no answer. He feels that same echoing void in his chest now too. Feels, maybe; or perhaps *felt*, because right now it feels like it is filling with a warmth that makes him feel uneasy.

"Maybe we were both born missing something," the Doctor says. "Or maybe it hadn't grown in yet. Maybe it's something, though, we can fix."

The Boy trembles, his jaundiced lips quivering. "What we've done can't be fixed," he says. "There are things that stay broken."

In the mirror, the Doctor sees himself above the half-made Boy, frowning down like a watchmaker unsure of whether he can reassemble the gear train. His shirtsleeves are bloody, his iron-gray hair is long and his beard unkempt. He looks old and tired. They both do.

"You are quite possibly correct." The Doctor looks down at the Boy. He rolls the Boy's neck to look at the damage to the stitches, but he can see the vein beneath is still pulsing. It's strong. "There are things we can't fix. But we must try."

The Parts of Him That I Can Help With

My younger brother Cameron never understood what working from home meant, so when he called me at 2:30 pm, I was wrist-deep in a twitching half-cadaver. Normally I wouldn't have answered, since I was practicing stitching a double set of lungs for an upcoming necromodding commission, but I'd been stymied by what to do next and I also had to pick Dylan up from school by 3:30, so it was as good a stopping point as any. Besides, what is family for if not to answer your call?

I pulled my hands out of the writhing thoracic cavity and peeled off my surgical gloves. The talc inside always makes me squirm when I rub my fingers clean, so I grimaced beneath my paper filtration mask—which I never remove while in my garage laboratory—and swiped my cell phone to speaker.

"Cam," I said. "What's up?"

"I need your help, bro."

"Are you drunk?" I asked.

He paused. "A little."

A little was fine. We're brothers, so how else were we supposed to talk?

"What's up?" I asked.

"Do you remember my last serious relationship?"

I had to think back. I was pretty sure that was Brandon, and that had been a year before? Two? Cam had never been good at relationships, but I'd forgotten how bad he was.

"Sure," I said. "Tall, dark, possibly rheumatic."

"You make him sound so sexy."

"Not my type."

"Anyway, I was out with Tyler."

"Who?" I asked as I walked across the room, away from the twitching body and the faint burning smell rising from the wires in its cranium.

"Never mind with who," Cam said, too quickly. "The point is that I ran into Brandon."

"With your car, I hope?"

"Nice dad joke, bro."

"Speaking of, I have to get Dylan soon." An hour wasn't really soon, but anything to give Cam a ticking clock. He's the kind of guy who if you ask him what he did last night, he'll end up telling you what he did this morning.

"Bro, this is serious," he said. "Seeing Brandon reminded me of how terrible I am at everything."

"What about this new guy?" I said, desperate to deflect the conversation. "Clearly you're not completely unlovable." Since launching my necromodding business, I'd had enough people calling me up for freebies that I was hoping to stem this off before it escalated. That double-lungs commission was the first paid job I'd had all month, although given how poorly it was going, I worried it might be the last too.

"It isn't going to work out," Cam said. "I'm not good enough."

"I'm not disagreeing," I said, but I immediately regretted that brotherly sarcasm as I heard a glass hit the bar on Cam's end. I could just about smell the booze through the phone. If I were there with him, maybe he could have seen on my face that I didn't mean it, but what could I say?

"I need your help to get a boyfriend," he said. "A serious one. A real one."

"One who calls you back?"

"One who thinks I'm hot."

"I don't know any blind and deaf guys," I said, unable to help ribbing him further. "Besides, I haven't dated anyone in, well, forever. I really can't help."

My wife, Cynthia, and I had been together basically forever. We'd dated for almost a decade, been married for something like seven years, and Dylan was five, so contemporary hook-up culture or any online presence more than my freelance necromodding website were absolute mysteries. Despite the skills at my disposal and the bodies in my garage, I didn't know what I could do to help Cam.

"Bro," Cam said, "I don't need your dating advice."

Oh thank god, I thought, although I was also a little offended.

"Then what?" I asked.

"I need to be a different person."

"Can't help you," I said. "Try therapy?"

"I mean, I need a new body."

The half-cadaver twitched on the table, the crown of electrodes in its skull stimulating it into smearing its coagulating intestines across the metal gurney as its torn throat wheezed through the half-sewn double-set of lungs. Seeing how helpless it was, twitching there in the approximation of life, made me feel bad that I hadn't had Cam over in a while.

"Fine," I said. "Come by tonight after dinner. No earlier than seven."

———

Cam arrived at 6:15. Cynthia was still cooking and I was helping Dylan with his enrichment homework when the doorbell rang. Cam tried the knob from outside, but I'd told Cynthia he was coming and so she'd locked it. She stood in the kitchen, stabbing me with her eyes as I walked Dylan to the door and unbolted it.

"Look who it is," I said to Dylan as we opened the door.

"Uncle Cam!"

As Cam hoisted Dylan up, I took a moment to do my pre-clinical once over. Cam and I shared a party mix of the same genetics, so I didn't think he'd been too let down, especially because if I'd received our parents' brain Chex, he'd gotten the pretzel bits of good physique. Decent shoulders and long arms, a full head of hair that was mostly not gray as he pushed into his thirties. While beer had softened him up, his spare tire was a bike wheel at worst, not a full radial. I was noting that his glutes were adequate if not extraordinary when I realized that he was airplaning Dylan into the kitchen with Cynthia.

"Hey, Cindy," he said, using a nickname she hates, perhaps accidentally.

"Hey, Ron," she replied, purposefully using a nickname Cam hates. "Can you not steer my child into the Bolognese?"

"Into the Bolognese!" Dylan squealed, and I could envision the downward arc occurring in the other room. Suddenly, I was hit by the pungent tomato sauce simmering over the sweet fat of the beef. It's funny how you don't recognize some comforts until you're just on their periphery.

"Ron," Cynthia said.

"Cindy," he said.

"Bolognese!" Dylan yelled.

I joined the family circle just in time and took Dylan from Cam's outstretched arms. Dylan pouted, but Cam ruffled his hair and then turned to me.

"So, what's for dinner?" Cam asked.

"Let's talk in the lab," I said, steering him toward the mudroom and the locked door to my lab in the garage. "We'll give Cynthia some room."

As Dylan latched onto Cynthia and I escorted Cam out, she gave me that look that asked, "Are you really skipping dinner?" I shrugged in apology and hoped my eyebrows, wriggling like caterpillars on a hotplate, said, "What else is family for, right?"

———

Out in the garage, the overwhelming smell of antiseptic spray is deceptive at first, but I offered a full respirator to Cam, which he wisely accepted. Whenever I open the storage drawers, the smell usually overwhelms the unprepared. It's the primary reason that Cynthia made me spring for airtight locks, because while she's fine with me being a stay-at-home dad doing freelance necromodder work, she doesn't want to be known as *that family*.

"How's business?" Cam asked, looking around at all the shiny equipment.

"Honestly, not great," I said. "It's really tough starting out. So far mostly just cranks and perverts."

"But this is all so, so cool," he said.

"Clients don't trust necromodders without a deep portfolio."

"I trust you, bro."

"You have to say that," I said, but I smiled beneath my paper mask. I didn't know if Cam was being sincere or just trying to butter me up, but it was working.

"What's that?" Cam asked, pointing to the halo of electrodes I'd been using to reanimate the half-cadaver with the double-stitched lungs. Cam had been in the lab enough to recognize new equipment, even though he didn't know what any of it was.

"Sort of a test drive system for bodies so I can try new mods before putting them in living clients," I told him. "The hope is to one day use it to amp up living brains, too, but that's a long way off." A very, very long way off, in fact, and not being able to get it to work stuck in my craw as yet another failure.

"No chance you can fix this then?" Cam thumped himself on the forehead.

"Nothing can fix that," I said. "What's Option B?"

"Bro," he said, "I need a boyfriend."

"Believe me," I said, "that would make all of our lives easier."

He ignored that comment, which was bigger of him than I expected. As the older brother, it was always both surprising and fulfilling to see sparks of maturity in Cam. Perhaps I sometimes pushed him too hard to find them—spraying his pants with water in middle school to teach him an ill-defined lesson about humility, for example—but whenever those moments emerged naturally, I could just about cry.

"I want someone to love me like Cynthia loves you," he said. I didn't tell him that sometimes it takes a lot of work, but I was a sucker for romance. If I could help him, at least a little, wasn't that my brotherly duty?

"So I need a new body," he said.

"It's expensive," I said.

"It can be my birthday present."

"It comes out of my pocket," I said, but Cam looked pointedly at me and I knew what he was being too nice to say about Cynthia in the other room. "Our pockets," I corrected myself. "Do you really want to take the Bolognese out of your nephew's mouth?"

"Birthday *and* Christmas."

I stared at him.

"For two years," he added.

I sighed. "And I can use pictures for my website."

"Fine," he said, "if I can also use them for my dating profile."

"Fine," I said. "I love—"

"Me?" Cam interrupted.

"A challenge," I concluded. "So, of course, I will help you."

There's a sort of code that we necromodders undertake—whether it's a full-time modder doing celebrity jobs in a fancy foreign clinic, or just a dedicated freelancer who left the hospital's daily grind and whose wife supports him while he builds up a portfolio on low-paying commissions—that we'll do our best to bring our clients' visions to fruition, despite our own preferences. I'd seen plenty of things on the professional message boards—literal eyes in the back of heads, third arms in places arms don't usually go—that I personally didn't think looked good, but which somehow made the end users feel complete. Although I think of necromodding as an art, most clients see it as design, so far be it from me to deny anyone their aesthetic preferences. As a medical professional, however, I did have one other complicating factor.

"I'll do it," I said, "but as your doctor..." I trailed off, hoping to prompt him.

"Really?" Cam asked. "Again?" He knew what was coming since I'd given him a new middle toe a year or so ago.

"Tell you what," I said as I punched in the codes to the cold storage. "If you can paraphrase the warning, I'll consider that informed consent."

"Let me see," Cam began as he joined me to watch the various hunks and chunks of cadavers slide out of the freezer. "As my doctor, you have to warn me of potential health effects related to body modifications using deceased tissue."

"And?"

"There's no guarantee."

"That?"

"That the process is effective or reversible."

"And?" I asked.

"And what?" he asked.

"You're of sound mind to make decisions that could result in your death."

He swallowed. "Yeah, bro."

From inside the coolers, corpses and extra bits peered out. I didn't keep a lot on hand, but I always had a few stock bodies—inoffensive types that were easy to cut and shape for after-market mods—so I could easily do a head swap, then touch Cam up afterward. With our health care system, there was never a shortage of parts.

"Finally," I added, "as your brother and not your doctor, I think you're great and have a great personality. Don't fix a thing, blah blah."

"I love you too, bro," he said.

"I never said that."

———

I cut off Cam's head and stitched it to the stock body that most closely matched his skin tone. He'd asked me about maybe trying out a different one, but that would just open up questions of bodily appropriation that I hadn't the energy to parse with Cam. Nevertheless, we had gone over the alterations he wanted and, once his original body was safely wrapped and secured in Refrigerator B and his head was hooked up to the new one, I was ready to start.

He wanted bigger muscles, and although the stock body was fairly normal, Cam had picked out globs of the red ropey fibers for me to put in. The sizing was ridiculous, but the more I'd warned him, the more he resisted. Then he said it was okay if I didn't know how to do it, which I'm pretty sure he did just to egg me on. Sure, a procedure of that level was just a smidge outside my comfort zone, but I wasn't going to give Cam the satisfaction of thinking he'd asked for something I couldn't do, so I went to work snipping out the default tendons at the muscle heads and reattaching bigger ones. It was like trying to overstuff a batch of viscera dumplings, but I finally got it done.

When I finished, I brought him back out from sedation and rolled the full-sized mirror over to where he lay on the table. He grinned and flexed, and I worried that the glue in the skin wouldn't hold, but although he bulged, he didn't pop. I'd had my doubts, but seeing it finished, I swelled with pride too.

"Isn't this a little excessive?" I asked, even as I snapped a picture for the portfolio section of my website.

"You just don't understand the male gaze," he said, and kissed his bicep.

"Come again?"

"Like, looking at stuff." He paused. "Also, that's what he said."

"That's so juvenile."

"You're the older brother," he said. "I'm not supposed to be too mature."

―――――

"I need to look more mature," Cam said, back in my lab after less than a week. "I have a baby face."

"You have a childish face," I said. I was already twisting his face this way and that under the light, though, figuring out what I could do with the soft tissues. Normally I wouldn't have been doing more work so soon after the first procedure, but working on Cam had really energized me. Prospective clients were contacting me and, in a spurt of inspiration, I'd finished the double-stitched lungs and even improved the corpse-animating electrode helmet. Besides, Cam seemed to enjoy coming over for the post-op check-ups, even sticking around to come with me to pick Dylan up from school.

"What do you want this time?" I asked.

"Thinner cheeks," he said. "And maybe a beard."

From Freezer A, I pulled out a box of frozen samples. Inside the compartments, little swatches of hair curled like sleeping gerbils in multiple hues of blonde, auburn, ginger, and black.

"You can have a beard of this, this, this, or this," I said, pointing out some.

"What about that?"

"That's a dog."

"That?"

"Pubes."

He considered it for a moment longer than I'd have liked, but then finally pointed to a nice normal brown swatch. "I'll take that one," he said.

"You sure?" I asked.

"Stop second guessing me."

So I put Cam under again. I made incisions beneath the zygomatic bones, then slit all the way down the jaw and back around. I took extra time to stencil out around Cam's lips before I peeled away his lower face, leaving him raw from closed eyes to throat. The yolk-colored globs of baby fat clung to his cheeks as I peeled them away, then laid them in the "Base" box to store in Freezer B alongside his original body. We were getting into alterations that weren't as simple to undo as a head swap, but I'd given him the spiel and, since he'd used up his allotment of gifts already, he'd promised to pay in cash—just later, of course.

I unfurled the main roll of beard and skin, measured off a swatch, and then snipped it. The surface was itchy and I couldn't imagine anyone wanting it on their face or anywhere else, but according to the message boards it was popular among other modders' clients and, of course, the customer is always right. It was a pain to smooth down and arrange all the follicles the right way, but it felt good getting into the granular work again. The bliss of losing myself in the details reminded me why I'd fallen in love with necromodding in the first place.

Once everything was perfect, I woke Cam up and rolled the mirror over. "This is good," he said, rubbing his new hirsute jawline while I took a picture for the site. "This will be the one that does it."

———

"The beard isn't doing it," Cam said at dinner. He'd shown up unannounced but had become a regular enough intrusion that Cynthia had a plate ready. He was still adjusting to his beard, though, and the egg from the fettuccine carbonara glistened in the hair.

"My problem is that I get too drunk," he said as he took another swig of Primitivo. He was still adjusting to the muscles, too, and so all of his movements were outsized and reckless. "I need the alcohol to open up, but then it hits me too hard."

"Drink less?" Cynthia recommended.

"Or he can give me a bigger liver," Cam said.

"An enlarged liver isn't healthy," I said. "It's pretty much the opposite."

"I know that," he said, although clearly he didn't. "Then give me more livers."

That might work and, if nothing else, would hopefully keep Cam away for a while. My work had been picking up recently—at first it was new clients looking for muscle and beard work after seeing Cam's pictures, but referrals and repeats kept rolling in. Besides, I'd been working on my electrode helmet and was on the verge of a breakthrough. Cam just didn't understand my need to work during the day or the importance of family time with Cynthia and Dylan afterward. His continued interruptions at dinner and frequent calls just to chat during the day were reminders as to why I'd stopped hanging out with him so much.

"Fine," I said to Cam. "Whatever you want."

After dinner, I took Cam to the lab and sliced him open, then clamped the flesh apart to root around. I wasn't shocked to see the paces he'd already put his current liver through. It looked scaled and pebbled, and oozed like a pickled beet. Even through my ventilator the rich, briny smell hit me. Gagging, I took the extra livers—my Burke and Hare men had been coming through like gangbusters recently—and started wedging them in. The healthy organs were more pliant, but as I sutured them together the knot of muscle got less and less manageable. In the end, I had to lean on them like I was packing a suitcase while I stapled the wound together. Despite being pleased with my innovation, this one wouldn't get a picture on the website. Probably just a text description.

As I brought Cam back around, I told him, "Be careful."

"I always am, bro."

He sat up on the gurney, swaying under the new imbalance.

"Should we do shots to celebrate?" he asked.

———

Cam banged on the front door on a Thursday night at 12:30 am. Cynthia and I were in bed, with Dylan down the hall asleep, and she was none too pleased at the interruption.

"He needs to learn boundaries," she said.

"I don't disagree," I said, but I was already out of bed and pulling on a robe. She wasn't wrong, of course, but it's hard to ignore family even when you want to. Besides, if I had to choose which one to deal with at that moment, Cam was probably the easiest.

Downstairs, I barely recognized Cam as I let him in. His body was getting strange; the muscles bulged in odd ways and all the livers seemed to be throwing him off balance. The beard hadn't been trimmed in days.

"Do you know what time it is?" I asked, dragging him into the garage laboratory. At least the insulated walls would keep his disturbance to a minimum.

"I need one last one," he said.

"Are you drunk?" I asked.

"Yeah," he responded. "So? You going to judge me for that too?"

"Someone has to."

"Too bad it isn't someone who ever has something nice to say."

That stung. It took me a moment to respond.

"I can't," I finally said. "It's too late."

"Please, I need it. You sort of owe me."

"For what?"

He didn't answer. "Just please. Do it and I'll leave you alone. Forever."

"Don't be such a martyr," I said.

"I just need you to make me taller, bro. Just an extra vertebra or three."

"You dope," I said. "It's not your height. It's not your muscles or your beard. It's just you."

"What do you mean?"

There are conversations that need to be had, and there are conversations that need to be had in a particular way. I knew this was the latter, but I was too tired. Besides, someone had to tell him, right?

"You're a weirdo," I said. "It's not how you look or how big your liver is; you're the kind of person who gets people's names wrong. You don't understand that you can't show up late or that you talk a lot or ask too much."

"Then fix that."

"I can't fix that," I said. "That's just you."

"Zap me then." He pointed at the electrode crown I'd been working on, the one that let me reanimate half-cadavers enough to test out mods before using them on paying clients. It had come a long way recently, and I was sure it was going to launch me out of necromods and into actual biomodding, but it wasn't ready to supercharge a living brain. Probably.

"It's untested," I said.

"I believe in you," he said.

"It's not about believing."

"I don't care," he snapped. "I already agreed you're not responsible if I die."

"You moron." I'd reached my limit, too. "Of course I'm responsible. I'm always responsible for you."

"Stop treating me like a child," he said. "If I could do this any other way, don't you think I would?"

What was there to say?

"Just zap me," he said again.

"Stop being so dramatic."

"I'm sorry I'm not perfect," he said. "Maybe if you didn't leave me behind after you went to school, after you got married, I could have learned from you."

"What was I supposed to do?" I asked.

"Help me," he said.

"I didn't leave you behind."

"I feel like you did."

"Fuck your feelings," I said.

We didn't talk as I put him under. Stewing, I drilled into his skull, then attached the headgear and pushed the little wire skewers in. That was it. If it killed him, well, I'd warned him, right?

I pulled the lever, hard. Because he'd asked for it.

The lights dimmed like I expected as it warmed up; but then it hitched. The lights flickered, then everything surged, bathing us in the miasma of green and red LEDs. All the shifting colors made me nauseous and I shaded my eyes, squinting at Cam's body under the waves of putrescent light.

Then it exploded.

Everything went black. As all the machines whirred to a stop, I couldn't hear or see anything. I sat there in the silent dark, wondering if I'd killed my brother. Wondering how I would explain it and wondering, afterward, just how much worse it could feel.

Those were my first thoughts. My next was that the brain-charger was also an obvious failure. My equipment was a failure. My skills were a failure. Sitting there, unable to see anything, the whole necromodding pursuit felt like a vain delusion. I was a dinner theater actor, alone in the dark among the empty tables and the cold buffet.

Then the red emergency lights came on, but all the monitors were still dead. I wondered if Cam was too. I couldn't bring myself to check for life the old-fashioned hands-on way, so I waited by the machinery. Maybe by refusing to check for myself, I could wait and blame the instruments.

It was the longest thirty seconds of my life.

Then the backup generator kicked on. One by one the monitors popped back up, flickering open like eyes. They ran through their reboots. Cam's heartbeat came up. His breathing levels stabilized. I brought him back around and he opened his eyes.

"What happened?" he asked.

"What do you think?"

He looked around at the red room and then down across his body and all the changes we'd been making.

"I gotta go," he said, sitting up. "I'm late."

And that was it. I glanced at the emergency report printouts and data, but I was too tired to deal with any of it, so I sealed the lab and went back to bed.

———

For the first day that I didn't hear from Cam, I was fine with it. I needed some space and figured he probably did too. I took Dylan to the park after school and just avoided the lab all together. After the second day without hearing from Cam, though, and then a third, I was worried. He didn't answer his phone. He didn't text me to ask for additional procedures or anti-rejection drugs. The kinds of modifications we had been doing had a fairly short active life without follow-ups.

I couldn't stop thinking about Cam. I'd really failed him, and not just as a necromodder—although that blow-up had me wondering if I should just give up, sell everything, and get a regular job again. No, I'd also failed Cam as a brother. It wasn't the things I'd said, since I stood by those, but that I'd said them in that way. That I'd made him feel that way. That he was willing to risk dying with my half-baked brain overcharger rather than have to deal with me as a brother anymore. That I'd been too proud or too stubborn to stop him. It was a dark time.

So I did what I always do when I have serious doubts and questions about life.

"What's going on?" Cynthia asked as she answered her cellphone. I'd expected her voicemail, but apparently I'd caught her in between meetings.

"It's Cam," I said.

"Not Dylan?"

"No," I said. "Cam."

She didn't hang up. She paused, but then continued: "What's wrong with your brother?"

"I don't quite know," I said. "I mean, I know you don't like him—"

"I like him," she cut me off. "I think you two have issues, but he's family."

"Right," I said.

"Your family," she said.

"Right."

We waited for a second there.

"What about him?" she broke the momentary silence.

"I'm worried," I said. "He hasn't called me since that last thing."

"Maybe it worked?"

"I don't think so," I said. "Regardless, there are these anti-rejection drugs that he knows he needs."

"Shit," Cynthia said.

"I know," I said. "What should I do?"

"Go find him, of course," she said.

I shook my head, even though she obviously couldn't see it. "He hasn't asked for my help."

There was silence on the other end. Then Cynthia said, softly, "What do you think all of this has been about, then?"

"I mean—" I began.

"Go help him!" Whatever pristine office halls she was in must have echoed, because the reverberation carried onto my end of the phone.

"But he might—"

"He's our family!"

She was right.

So I drove to Cam's apartment complex on the other side of town. I'd been there a few times before to pick him up for family events or to visit someone in the hospital, but it took some poking around and checking mailboxes before I found his building again. The door to his unit was unlocked, yet even before I entered, I could smell the rot.

Cam was sitting in the dark, sagging in the center of his rent-to-own couch. The putrescence seeping out from around his midsection was soaking into the fabric. The muscles I could see—biceps, triceps, traps, and pecs—were purple and mustard-yellow clots beneath the skin. The edges of his beard were peeling down.

"Hey," he said.

"Hey," I said. "Let's get you back to the lab."

"It's not worth it."

"Don't start," I said. "Not now." I picked my way around empty silver tallboys swimming like fish on the stained blue carpet.

"I've just been thinking," he said. "I can't do anything but think after what you did."

"I didn't do anything," I said. I grabbed his arm and began to pull, but it was slack and, without his assistance, I worried my fingers would sink in and tear out big chunks.

"You broke my brain, bro," he said, and sunk down deeper. "All that zap did was make me depressed."

"The machine didn't do that, you dolt," I said. It was true: when I'd reviewed the data that night, it was clear that the machine hadn't worked. It had fried during the warm-up and, although it blasted everything in the lab, there'd been no sign that it had any effect on Cam. "If you're thinking about how shitty things are, then that's on you."

He had nothing to say to that.

I sighed. "And on me, too. I guess."

Cam grunted.

"I'm sorry I said those things. For now, though," I said, "as your doctor, I need to get you back to the lab before you have catastrophic organ failure." I pulled again but although he didn't actively resist, he didn't move his bulk to accommodate me either.

"What do you want from me?" I finally asked.

"You could tell me you love me."

"Well, I won't do that," I said. "But, as your doctor—as your brother—I'd be pretty upset if you had catastrophic organ failure."

———

The lab door is triple-sealed so that smells don't seep into or out of the house, which is why it wasn't until Cam and I opened the door that the wave of rot pushed out past us. The sweet and sick burst curled into my nostrils and even Cam—decaying from the neck down—winced at the ripe odor.

We stumbled into the lab, but I already knew what had happened. The power surge had blown the freezers and they hadn't reset with the other equipment. When I opened Freezer B, as the smell had foreshadowed, everything was ruined. Cam's original body was beyond salvage.

"I'm so sorry," I said.

Somehow in this tragedy, Cam had found equanimity and so he shrugged, one of the seams around his neck popping loose and green pus oozing out. For a moment, I felt that swell of pride in how mature he was acting.

We moved over to the table and I sat him down. All of my lab equipment seemed to be working fine, but there was nothing in the freezers I could use. What a pair our mismatched reflections in the full-length mirror made—me standing there slicked with gore, and my younger brother falling apart like a poutine. I was trying to be strong, holding it together, but then Cam had to go and get sentimental.

"It was really nice spending time with you," Cam said. "But I feel like you'll be better off without me."

"I never wanted to lose you," I said. "I just wanted, you know, less of you."

"Well, you're in luck. There isn't much left." He tried to laugh, gesturing to the pile of meat festering below his neck.

"Oh shit," I said.

"What?"

"There might be a way." *Less of him.* "It might be too complicated, though. I don't know if I can do it."

"Bro," he said, and flopped a mushy hand onto my shoulder. "I believe in you."

"You kind of have to say that," I said, wrestling the tears back as best I could.

"Maybe," he said. "But I feel like you know it's true."

I sniffled, just once. "Fuck your feelings."

Then I cut off Cam's head.

———

"Swipe right," Cam said.

"Don't yell in my ear," I said.

"I'm not yelling."

"Well, it sounds like it."

That was because his head was attached to my shoulder, so his mouth was right next to my ear. Normally he didn't get this excited, but while we were sitting at the dinner table with Dylan, waiting for Cynthia, Cam had decided he absolutely needed to show me this new dating app. I didn't really want to see, but I'd been trying to be more supportive lately. It was his life, after all. Mostly.

Cam whispered: "Swipe right."

"Fine," I said. "But I'm not taking you on any dates. Wait until your replacement body gets in."

"Then I'm not doing any more surgeries with you."

That wasn't okay. Ever since I'd posted about our successful head graft, the commissions were rolling in. Not only that, but with Cam by my side, I finally felt like a true professional.

"Fine," I said. "But just one date. Make it count."

"Fine," he said. "Now swipe right."

I swiped right and the next image popped up. I gasped.

"Can I see?" Dylan asked from across the table.

"No!" Cam and I shouted in unison.

Cynthia came out of the kitchen, carrying a bowl of salad. "No phones at the table," she said.

"Sorry, Cynthia," Cam said. Over the past week, he'd been making a real effort to get her name right and to be a better houseguest in general. For her part, Cynthia had been much more understanding about all of this than I'd had any right to expect. Of course, she rightly insisted that Cam and I sleep on the couch downstairs. It's funny, but you never realize how much you might miss some people until you're just on their periphery, I guess.

"Dinner time is family time," Dylan chimed in.

"That's right," I said, but as I went to put the phone in my pocket it rang, playing "Sunshine of Your Love."

"Whose ringtone is that?" Cynthia asked.

"Tyler," I said, reading off the Caller ID.

"Who's Tyler?" Dylan asked.

I suddenly felt light-headed as the blood from my body rushed to Cam's face. He'd turned bright red and I felt the heat of his ear next to mine. I worried for a moment that our sutures might spring a leak.

"Just some guy I was seeing before all this," he said. He swallowed and the movement of his esophagus shook my collarbone.

"Just some guy, Cam?" Cynthia said. "I've never seen you this flustered."

"I'll call him later," Cam said. "Dinner time is family time." I could feel him straining, though, as he looked at the phone. I admired his attempt at impulse control, but then I looked at Cynthia and she smiled wearily.

"What else is family for?" she said.

"No, really," Cam said. "It's okay. I—"

I swiped the phone open and held it to Cam's ear. I rose from the table and as we walked out Cam began, adorably, to stutter a hello.

Cynthia was right: What else is family for, of course, if not to answer your calls?

From October Vines

~ Cordials and Port ~

If you speak a word, the spell is broken. This is the first rule of a dumb supper.

So you walk silently backward up the steps from the unkempt lawn to the sagging porch, Madison behind you going first to open the door and Selene in front, bringing up the rear. Cheeks pouched, lips pursed, each of you carries a tray covered with a white dust cloth into the old house.

Through the foyer, up the grand staircase, you three walk backward, dragging your heels so as not to trip on the steps. You watch the back of Selene's head, the collar of her pale dress. You listen for the brush of Madison's hem when she reaches the landing. Down the hall, then, still hesitant as warped boards under damp carpet bend beneath your feet. Moonlight through the great window's empty panes paints everything blue and black except your white dresses and the cloth over your trays.

Then Madison stops. The door behind you groans open into the room you girls had set for supper earlier that afternoon. That was back when there was light and you could speak.

Madison, you, Selene: in that order, you back into the room. The round table at the center has no cloth, but bears a clutch of dead candles and eight full place settings with seven empty chairs. The seat closest to the door, however, is already occupied.

Regina, completely covered by the thick white sheet, waits. Stiff linen creases pool shadows along the hollows of her face beneath and, in the dimness, her features are melting like wax.

Then Madison strikes the match. As candlelight fills and softens the pits of Regina's shroud, you can almost imagine that what lies beneath is furniture or a sack of laundry. But comfort is fleeting.

The inside of your closed mouth is beginning to burn; your tongue is numb and your gums prickle. The cool sting of alcohol swells with every inhalation through your nostrils as they are tickled, too, by dust and the first bloom of rot. So the three of you set your covered favors on the table and seat yourselves in predetermined order. Clockwise, it runs: Regina, empty, Madison, empty, Selene, empty, you, empty. Regina's sheet glows against the void of the door directly behind her.

Madison nods to Selene, Selene to you, you to Regina. Regina doesn't move.

Before each of you is a place setting done in mirror. Spoons and knife on left, forks on right. Bread plate and dinner spoon hover between empty glasses for water, wine, and after-dinner drinks on the table's edge.

Madison lifts her smallest glass, and you and Selene follow. You raise them to your lips and spit back the liqueur you have been holding without swallowing since you first crossed the threshold. The liquid is dark amber and bubbled with saliva, but its ghost still coats your mouth like sap.

You place your glasses down. The dumb supper has begun.

———

You took the crooked steps two at a time and the landing at a sprint. Still, when you reached the room—the round table already draped in white linen and ringed by eight empty chairs—Madison's shriek had collapsed into sobbing. Selene stared open-mouthed.

Framed by a panel of setting sunlight through the window, Regina lay. Her eyes were bulged by broken capillaries, her tongue swollen, her throat clawed and bruised. Her honeyed ringlets spilled out like an illumination of the soul rising from the dead.

Although the dumb supper was yet hours away, none of you spoke.

~ Dessert ~

The dessert course is Selene's. Seated opposite and furthest from Regina, she is still in shock after finding the body. She bears the same wide-eyed, unseeing disbelief as when Madison first lumbered the corpse into the chair and covered it with the tablecloth. Even now, Madison has to wave multiple times before Selene registers that it is time.

Had it gone as expected, the dumb supper would have been simple. You would do it backward; you would do it in silence; you would do it on Samhain. One by one, each girl would be joined by an apparition of her husband-to-be. That had been the plan.

Selene uncovers the dish before her: German chocolate cake. She takes up the gleaming pie-knife's wedge, then turns it backward, gripping the blade. With the handle, then, Selene furrows out eight mangled portions. One by one, plates are passed and she shovels out the moist crumb like mud in the candlelight. Dessert is placed in front of every seat. The three of you raise the littlest spoons.

A dumb supper, in truth, is not so universally simple. In some places, the empty seats are reserved for spirits. In others, it foretells if you will die. Here, tonight, you three who remain believe it might reveal who killed Regina. This is why Madison insisted on proceeding.

So you take a bite of the ruined cake, the sweetness piling over top of the liqueur's still-sweet residue on your tongue. The steady slog of chewing pulses through your jaw, jostling the mouse bones in your ears and burying all other sounds except the whistle through your nose. You are watching Selene in the middle of your second mouthful, however, when her eyes go wide and her face drains. This freezes you, and then you hear what she hears.

In the hallway, something heavy is approaching. A pulsing drag, pause, drag, pause, grows louder as it reaches the black of the door behind Regina. A drag, then a pause just outside the frame.

An enormous worm's glistening pink head pokes inside, large around as your thigh. In the candles' flicker, you see bits of loam clinging to its reticulations like morsels of German chocolate cake. Neither Selene, nor Madison, nor you make a sound as the worm inches in, around the table clockwise and toward Madison, who remains still.

It crawls past Madison, then rears up to squirm onto the seat between her and Selene. Selene begins panting around her mouthful of cake, hyperventilating as the chair on her right creaks beneath the worm's weight and it loops one kink of itself around the headrest to assume a seated position. She is about to scream and break the spell, despite Madison's furious waving entreaties, when the thing happens.

The worm parts its lips to reveal a set of yellowed teeth, as broad and flat as ivory dentures. It pulls its skin's edges back into a smile, then dips down to gnash at the chocolate cake before it.

———

Bradley must have known why you were walking down the road with a salad bowl. The old house was the only thing out that way.

He smiled, leaning from his car window. "Have you seen Regina?"

It was a casual question made strange by the distance from any explanation for his presence. A boyfriend's bored curiosity? Jealousy?

He grinned again, batted his lashes. Your heart fluttered and you felt sick. You shook your head, No.

"Is she up at that house?" he asked. "Are you girls doing something naughty? Should I go take a look?"

You shook your head again.

~ Entree ~

Without looking at the worm to her left or Selene sobbing one seat past, Madison prepares to reveal the entree. She and Regina, it seems, were the best friends and the circle's center. Selene, you had suspected and have now confirmed, was merely an extra spoke to help the wheel turn.

You are not unsympathetic. You already knew that Selene would die unmarried. You didn't need the dumb supper for that.

Madison draws back the white cloth from the tray before her, untenting a roast chicken already stripped to the bone. It verges on a surgical marvel how cleanly she has pared the flesh away, as if an anatomical diagram, blown out and the minutiae labeled, has fallen onto a silver platter.

As Madison reconstructs the chicken slice by slice for serving, Selene weeps openly without speaking, chocolate dessert crusted at her mouth's corners. The shovel-toothed worm, too, has pieces caked in its crevices but otherwise grins eyeless at its empty plate.

By the time Madison has reassembled her Faberge roast, there is a creaking on the grand stairs. As she serves it like a jigsaw, the footsteps creep across the landing. The hall. Outside the door. You look up as your plate reaches your hand. A man-sized and man-shaped shadow looms behind Regina's shroud before the door.

Bradley, in a form, half-steps into the room. There is a dizziness to his features, a mélange of his eyes and mouth and a shifting of his limbs. It is not so much that he cannot settle on which way to stand, but more that reality has not yet settled on which of the overlapping versions of him stands there. Selene, poor girl, does not respond at all. Madison, however, stares, mouth agape, and then turns to you. Her eyes ask, without speaking, if you have been found out. Then, the alternative blossoms: Is this what you have conducted the dumb supper to discover? Was it him?

As Madison stares at you over the worm, which delicately nibbles a drumstick with its outsized teeth, you watch the swirl of Bradleys in the doorway split like oil on water. The inaccuracy of his features, the almostness of his gaze, everything resolves as the solid part—the real Bradley—falls back and staggers off down the hall. Down the stairs. The door slams below.

The aspect of Bradley which remains is a gossamer boy, a thin and diaphanous fancy. He smiles so wide, but his eyes are empty and have no lashes to bat. With silent steps, the ghost of him skirts to Regina's right and sits down in the empty chair between you two.

Smiling blankly, the specter saws away at the ghost of the chicken with transparent versions of his offhand silver.

Madison stares at you. Her eyes are saying, I told you, I knew it was him. She tilts her head to the door, questioning. But you shake your head.

You sweep a hand to the remaining dumb supper before you. The spell can't be broken before it ends.

———

"Food comes last, stupid," Regina said. "You know that."

Your cheeks burned as she laughed. You picked up your covered bowl, but Regina grabbed your wrist. "Don't," you would have whispered, but you held still as her dusty fingers slid up under the sheath and plucked out a round, ripe tomato. Past her fine lips, she popped the fruit between her teeth.

"You're leaving me to set up alone?"

You opened your mouth as if to answer, but she waved you off as she wiped the juice from her lips' corner.

"Maddy and Selene are coming soon. Don't bother hurrying."

~ Salad ~

You cannot put tomatoes back on the vine. You cannot plant cabbage back in the soil or re-stem spinach. What is done cannot be undone; what is seen, not unseen; said, not unsaid. You wonder, as you unveil your salad with the crisp bed-lettuces and jewel tomatoes, if the others appreciate this.

You have only dipped the tongs hinge-first into the bowl when the first cavernous thump resonates downstairs. Even poor Selene stirs momentarily from her horror and the worm beside her quivers, its attention drawn. Only phantom Bradley beside you continues to eat his ghostly meal uninterrupted.

Madison looks to you, the fear in her eyes almost a delicacy. Your cheeks flush to think that you are the expert here. Then you realize she is focused on phantom Bradley to your left. Has she put together that at the dumb supper the seats are reversed from custom, with the woman on the right and her date—or fate—on the left? That this makes Bradley yours and not Regina's? But does she really think you would entertain such a union? Well, yes, he's rich. Handsome, too, perhaps. But none of this is where your interest lies as the dumb supper approaches its conclusion.

You flap out the green leaves and ruby tomatoes alongside juicy cucumbers and crumbled feta. No dressing, of course, as you couldn't jury-rig it back into the bottle. Your aim now is to serve everyone before the drumming on the stairs arrives.

Since there are only two seats left—the empty one to Regina's left beside Madison, and the one right between you and Selene—Madison takes her plate and rakes her salad in with a knife. Selene and the monstrous worm grind face-first at their plates, mindless, as the intruding guest's heavy step resonates down the hallway.

With everyone else chomping away, you take the final plate as the approaching clomp reaches the hallway's end. Madison and Selene and the worm roar through their courses, as if finishing before the new attendant can assume his spot might prevent his arrival. You, however, place yours down with the leaves and glistening tomatoes untouched. The others have too much left to eat, anyway, and cannot wipe away the juice from the last ripe tomatoes fast enough as the behemoth enters.

It is an enormous coffin, covered in dirt. It wobbles from end to end into the room under its own power. A gentleman obelisk, it waits at the threshold for just a moment. A heavy breathing rocks the lid out and in. Then it wobbles in, step by half-step, three inches at a time. The wheezing ebony casket stumbles around the table, past the empty chair between Regina and Madison. Madison. The worm. Selene.

Then, with a ponderous inhale, it collapses toward you but you don't even flinch as only inches away it crushes the chair between you and Selene into splinters.

The wobble of the table sends cold salad tumbling across its face.

————

Fresh from October vines, you ran the tomatoes beneath the kitchen tap and placed them on the terrycloth towel to dry before adding them to the salad. Undressed, obviously.

"I don't know why you're doing this with them," your brother called from the living room. "Bradley, Regina's boyfriend, says they say you're weird."

You knew that. But you also knew they thought you knew weird things too. Things like the dumb supper.

And you do. But you know better ones too.

You inserted the hypodermic needle through the tomato's skin, just a perfect little hole, and plumped it full and juicy.

~ Aperitif ~

Aperitif was to be Regina's, but your digestifs sit there, waiting. This is the dumb supper; the end is the beginning.

Poor Selene, already drained, died almost immediately. Draped across her coffin, her cooling weight keeps the lid from rattling. The worm, too, is slung over its headrest, purpling and tumescent as poison courses through its single vein. Madison, though, still thrashes willfully on the floor. She claws her throat as if to open it for air and, wildly flailing, grips the cloth covering Regina. She yanks it away to reveal Regina—the first and now final unveiling —yawning as wide and empty as the doorway beyond.

Soon enough, however, even Madison stops moving.

Alone, you lift your aperitif, having come full circle. The liquid is still dark amber, pearlescent with saliva bubbles. You are contemplating its viscosity when the last guest appears.

You.

The you who enters is thin and gauzy, like Bradley's specter still blithely smiling on your date-side. You try to wave your doppelgänger away; the party is already over and the killer revealed. Nevertheless, it seats itself on Regina's body's left.

Hollow-eyed and grinning, your ghost is sitting politely when the first splash of crimson light soaks the room. It washes ruby red, then bruise blue, then repeats. You rise and approach the window. Down below is a police car, lights flashing but siren off.

Two officers emerge and open the back to release their passenger. It's Bradley: the real Bradley, not your ghostly companion who split off from him when he intruded during the entree course. Your killer, then, and not your husband. You sigh. That makes more sense.

He points up to where the window frames you, so you smile and wave. As the officers stare, hands on holstered pistols, you raise a toast, the liqueur alternating red and blue as if unsure of its final form. Then you turn back to the dumb supper's remains.

Downstairs, the front door is kicked in. When they reach this room, the spell will be over, so you prepare. As they gallop up the grand stairs, you blow out the candles. As they reach the landing, you pick up a fork and spear one perfect tomato from your salad plate. In the flashing light it is the most brilliant red, then the dullest gray, blinking like an eye.

The men are racing down the hall as you hand your ghost the fork. The first officer inside tackles your double from its chair just as it bites down. Bradley and the other officer, taking in the full carnage, blanch. You smile and throw back your aperitif.

Your own deal is concluded, your spell completed.

You are vibrating. You are transforming. Darkness consumes you and then you are darkness. You are more powerful, less defined, than anything Regina, Madison, Selene, Bradley, or anyone else could have imagined.

In the gap between red and blue, you slip out through the darkness into the night. You spread your wings.

———

You were pruning vines when the darkness spoke to you again from the shadows beneath the leaves. You pretended not to hear.

Regina, Madison, and even Selene had ditched you again. But it was fine, you lied; more time to attend to these withered stalks. Your tomatoes were still unripe, but without the leeches they might be salvageable.

The darkness called you by name and you clipped a bit too far, nicking your fingertip.

"What do you want?" you hissed.

Your brother slid open the side door. "Telephone," he called out. "It's those girls."

"You," the darkness answered.

Fine and Fancy Arms

My grandma told me that before Great-Uncle Harwin passed, Jesus save him, his parsimoniousness was such that he lived at the bottom of the steepest hill in Mosby County so that he wouldn't have to use the extra gas driving home from the mill each night. He would jimmy the engine off when his one headlight hit the crest, downshift the mushroom-gray primer-patched Ford into neutral, and coast the decline to where his red dirt drive began and then in as far toward his home as he could before it rolled to a stop and he walked the rest. The only cent he ever spent on that truck, leaving aside the afternoon he bought it at a bank foreclosure auction on the Mosby Courthouse steps, was when he had Walter Hern in Statesville County jury-rig it so that Harwin could drive despite his double arm prostheses.

The branch of my family on which Harwin was but one bud had, for many years, been renowned in Mosby County as water witches. Not every one of them, of course, but more of the boy children could than couldn't hold onto a forked rod of beech or peach, or even applewood, and dowse out at least some kind of water. Even when Harwin was a small boy—back when he was so apple-cheeked and freckled that his own mother had a heart attack when she mistook him for an enormous ladybird coming through the tobacco leaves one bright noon—the witching was particularly strong in him. Branches would writhe and whip in his hands, dancing like a chicken in church until, *bam*, right down into the ground. Sure as spit, there'd be water.

And so, Grandma told me, between the novelty of his round, red cheeks, and the uncanny consistency with which working wells were dug at his direction, young Harwin became quite a cause célèbre. He was ferried all around the eastern counties in a mule cart to raise water for the farms from Mosby to Statesville to Dutch to Degram. At age eleven, he was summoned halfway across the state to the Governor's Mansion for a commendation where Governor Ledsome himself pinned a little medal with the State Seal on Harwin's lapel and handed him a handsome silver-painted stick while the press bulbs flashed. When Harwin's father found out the photograph was going to run in the city paper the next weekend, he drove all the way back out across the state again on Sunday, only to find it had run in the Saturday Post and not a copy was left for any price. The loss of that paper haunted Harwin's father, not in the least because it had been the last photograph taken of the boy with his original arms.

What happened next is, as my grandma would say, uncertain. Mosby County, son of sharecropper—there's no immediate reason to assume that Harwin's mangling must have involved foul play. Mowers, tractors, threshers, bailers, harrows, buggies, feral pigs. An eleven-year-old boy could lose his arms on any day that ends in Y, although, Grandma would also grant you, losing both at once was a bit unusual.

But here's what I've heard, when my second cousin has been deep in the mash and decides he wants to tell me the real story. He says that it was a pack of jealous boys from the next farm over, who finally tired of rosy-cheeked Harwin and his silver stick and his little medal getting all the attention. They dragged him to the edge of the thresher's great grinding maw, just to put the fear into him, of course. But a slip, though—or even a push, perhaps—and that was that. Left arm gone just above the elbow; right arm, just below.

I've heard the same story from my second cousin's half-sister—well, almost just the same—but she told that it was Harwin's father who had grown tired of all the boy's attention. Another version involves the Noon-witch, but even I won't speak of her and her teeth like porcelain spades.

Whatever way it came to pass, beyond his arms, Harwin lost so much blood that his round, red cheeks drained out like wineskins, leaving the slack and pasty jowls that hang-dogged him for the rest of his life. How he made it to the hospital the next town over was in the back of the hay wagon, the ragged ends of his arms tourniqueted off but still bleeding through the straw until it stuck to his stumps like red and golden feathers. How he made it through the night, well, that was a miracle. When he returned to Mosby County six weeks later, he was wearing welfare-issue arm prosthetics—two sizes too big, with rough leather cuffs and rusty hooks. People saw him walking, crestfallen, heavy wood and wire arms dragging in the dirt, hunched like a swayback mule under the weight.

Such indignity, of course, could not be abided. Everyone across the eastern counties had a story about young Harwin, and so they came together to do him a charity. Donations were collected by the Mount Zion Baptists, the First Free Will Baptists, the Free First Will Baptists, and even the Church of the French Jesus, which bore that unfortunate appellation due, rightly or wrongly, to a perceived metropolitan character imparted by the swept tips on their stained-glass Messiah's otherwise pencil-thin mustache. Regardless, they collected enough to commission little Harwin a set of willow wood arms—light and thin, but beautiful. Willow wood isn't a strong material, the craftsman warned them, but it was the general consensus there wasn't much work Harwin would be doing.

The arms were delivered to the pastor and they were fine indeed. However, the church elders couldn't agree on when or how or at which church to present them to Harwin—although they all agreed the French Jesus was out, and even its leaders didn't disagree—and so they waited until the Mosby County Fall Fair, so that they could bring him up on the outdoor stage and all "give him a hand." The pastor had been particularly pleased with that little jest. Then, there in front of God and everyone from Mosby County—and some from Statesville, Degram, and Dutch, too

—they strapped the fine willow wood arms onto the sad, pale boy. The pastor shook his right wooden hand and Harwin stared at it as if he couldn't quite understand the thing, while all the assembled crowd stood beaming at him, waiting for the outpouring of gratitude. My grandmother, a girl then, was in that crowd, and she remembered how they waited. And they waited.

Then Harwin's new right hand shot out as if he were waving hello to someone in the wings. The pastor dodged back as Harwin's left followed, swooping in an arc before crooking at a mad angle. Murmuring, the crowd watched as little Harwin followed some unseen attention, clomping across the boards, new willow arms waving out in front as if pulled by invisible marionette strings that stretched up to great hidden hands in the sky. The pastor, still waiting for his thanks, followed.

Harwin stumbled down the stage steps and then bowed deeply, arms touching the ground, and the crowd gave a smattering of confused applause, but then he swung back up. In his right willow hand, a small fold of money was pinched between the stiff fingers. The smattering of applause increased accordingly. Patting his pockets, the pastor descended from the stage and took the clip from Harwin's outstretched prosthetic.

"Why, this is mine," the pastor cried. "I must have dropped it on the way to the stage, but the boy's arms felt it when we shook and then found it. Truly this is the prosperity of the Lord! Give unto the least of you, and you shall receive."

The assembled county men and women roared, the meaty smacking of their palms a veritable storm. The pastor took Harwin's still-extended hand and lifted it as if he was declaring the victor of the Annual Sack Race, but Harwin's fine willow arm twisted and jerked, pulling free. With another reeling lurch, arms windmilling, Harwin was out into the grass, then off toward the barns set up for displays of odd-sized livestock and produce. The pastor and all of the crowd followed a few steps behind, breaths held and waiting.

Harwin stopped momentarily, then tipped over as the hands swung down to a tuft of grass. The left one arose, fingertips pressed like a bird's bill, with a small gold band bit between them. The pastor stepped forward and, with some effort, pried the discovery loose.

"A ring," he said to the crowd. "Blue stones, set three in a row." He turned it around, peered inside. "An inscription?"

Ms. Maybelline Harp pushed her way to the front. "Does the inside say, *Let not the waters rise*? Oh please, Pastor."

He confirmed it did and Maybelline broke into sobs. "That was my mother's ring, and she lost it here at the fair three years ago."

The crowd *Amen*-ed and *Hallelujah*-ed, and the pastor reached once more for Harwin's hand, but warily this time, and with good cause, for the now the boy's willow arms threw themselves back toward the barns and Harwin practically tore off after them. Everyone followed at a run—women hiked their skirts, gentlemen mopped their brows, the children whooped and hollered—and all the while poor, pale-cheeked, fine-armed Harwin ran toward the animal barn where the prize-winning livestock had all been gathered earlier that evening for the ribbon ceremony.

Into the barn he flew, and then stopped. Not everyone in the crowd would fit, of course, and the pastor had to elbow his way inside. There they all stood waiting as, hands raised and fingers spread like he was warming them before an unseen fire, the boy perambulated the enclosure, holding them up to each animal, one by one, just a few inches away from their skin. First, Judd Brumb's award-winning heifer. Then Mrs. Richard Cleave's rabbit, which had earlier been crowned the largest in the counties. Then all of the Lewis family's Polish chickens, bobbing their tufted feather wigs under the scrutiny. Then to Gaith Mathel's blue-ribbon sow, the tallest and fattest that had been entered in fifteen years. Harwin stopped before the pig.

Holding out his wooden hands, eyes closed in studious concentration, the boy seemed to be reading a kind of magnetic braille that hovered over the pig. It was clear by now that whatever witching he had employed through the mere dowsing rods was amplified by the replacement of his arms. Already he had found a dropped billfold, a ring lost for years, and now this. Whatever this was.

Gaith Mathel's pig was a monstrous thing. Pale pink, so fat that its eyes had sunken away, covered from dripping snout to crusty haunch with blonde bristles that held the chaff from the hay bedding. On its flanks, large blue-gray birthmarks marred it like mud that wouldn't wash off.

"Keep that armless bastard away from her!" Gaith called out, pushing toward the front.

But he couldn't get through the wall of attentive bodies; not before Harwin's willow hands once more swooped down and came to rest on the pig's massive flank. At first, it seemed like a muscle tremor or maybe flatulence, rippling the pig's hide, but as the crowd watched, the blue-gray birthmarks began to move across the skin. They swirled together, coalescing like a movie being projected on the screen of the pig, until they formed a woman's face.

"Oh, thank the Lord!" the face on the pig's side said, and more than one delicate soul in the crowd swooned. "It's dark in here, and I fear my husband has done something terrible!"

Then the face began to scream, and the pig squealed and shat, and the fine willow hands flew down once more, this time arising with a half-digested finger bone from the pile of excrement. The pastor fainted, and the men in the crowd grabbed Gaith Mathel, and the blue-gray face on the side of the pig kept screaming for a whole day until the police shot the pig dead and had Tom Zicker, the butcher, dig what was left of Gaith Mathel's wife, who was meant to be visiting relatives one state over, out of the sow's intestines. After that evening at the Mosby County Fall Fair, Great-Uncle Harwin was once again a cause célèbre.

In the years that followed, dowsing work was steady pay for Harwin. No longer limited to just the eastern counties, folks from all over the state would pay to have him carted out and waltzed across the fields, waving his arms above their farms to point out where to dig. There was a system, Grandma said, with respect to how many fingers on which hand were extended times a number based on which of the other hand's fingers were curled plus some other factor, but, well, Grandma would have been the first to tell you she hadn't a head for numbers. The point was if a digger did the math, he knew exactly how far below the sod the water sat. It was a sight to see, I hear, and Harwin's trips became events, until he was fed proper and put up in every town that needed a well or a pump or just a good show. He filled out as he grew up, although his pale jowls, drained of blood when he lost his arms, remained flaccid throughout his life.

If dowsing water was steady, honest work that kept Harwin's family fed, it was the other sort of witching that put money in his own pockets and made him fat. It began with finding the odd lost watch or heirloom brooch, something he did for the farmers when he was already out at their farms, but there are other people for whom gold and silver is worth more than water. Not infrequently, long black cars were spotted cruising through Mosby County in the evening like gar through the still waters of Cotner's Creek, ferrying young Harwin to and fro on less public errands. Part of his payment was for discretion, I imagine, and so I have only rumors to relay—a wealthy patriarch who passed and the only copy of his will misplaced; a money box blown clear when an outhouse distillery exploded; more than one coot's buried treasure after he was too addled to recall where it'd been hid. It was even said that some mysterious benefactors staked Harwin a few times to go down to Waller's Hollow—Waller's Holler, as it was known back then—for days at a time to search the swamp, grid by grid, in search of that fabled cache of Confederate gold. I do not believe he ever found it, but I do believe he was rewarded handsomely for trying.

So it was that in the sixteenth summer of Harwin's life, four years into witching with the willow arms which had by then become dinged and scratched through constant vigorous use, Great-Uncle Harwin, flush with pocket money, commissioned himself a pair of fine and fancy arms of his own design. He had them made one each of beech and peach, inlaid with little strips of ash and copper bands. They were wondrous, and whether they worked better than the willow or just looked it, Harwin's lot continued to improve.

In his sixteenth year, he also bought the family an automobile. In his seventeenth year, he bought a new house for his family on their own plot of land. In his eighteenth year, early one evening as the first crisp autumn breeze was tugging the first orange leaves from the Mosby County elms, a long black car arrived to summon Harwin once again to the Governor's Mansion. This time, he knew, there was likely no commendation, but the allure of silver that wasn't just a painted stick was too much for him to refuse.

The car arrived at the Mansion sometime between midnight and morning, while it was still dark out and the gas lamps by the gateway bathed everything in an unusual glow. Fall had settled on the governor's grounds early, and in the moonlight the trees were already red and brown and partially bare, like hands reaching out of the earth. The driver did the roundabout and let Harwin out by the grand entrance where the butler, an elderly manservant with a stiff back and one mustard yellow eye, was already waiting. Harwin was groggy and his mouth was sticky, having slept fitfully along the ride, but the butler shooed Harwin up the steps to the enormous front doors, which opened as he approached.

"Welcome," said Governor Ledsome. He was a tall man, barrel-chested, with more iron in his mustache than he'd had when Harwin had been here so many years before, but he wore his age well. Beside him stood his brother, an official of some rank in the governor's cabinet, and the spitting image of his brother—if the spit had bubbled and slid a bit where it'd been spat.

"You are here to find an ill spirit that has been deviling us," the governor's brother said. The brother was an older, more bulbous version of the governor, and he leaned heavily on two thick hickory canes with silver dog's heads for handles. His left foot was wrapped in loose bandages, bare toes sticking out and red as coals. He winced at the slightest shift.

Harwin shook his head and tried to apologize. Ever since the incident with Gaith Mathel and his pig, Harwin's father had forbade him from witching out spirits and haints. Of course, he didn't mind working Harwin to splinters on the dowsing rounds and would turn a blind eye to the more suspect requests his son fetch a "lost" object, but spirits were the line that could not be crossed. Harwin, eighteen and alone in the Governor's Mansion, meant to hold firm and respect his father's wishes, Jesus love him. He made it five whole minutes until the governor's brother sighed in evident disgust and, without any negotiation, named a price that dropped Harwin's jaw so low that even his saggy jowls went taut. Harwin and the governor shook hands, hot flesh and cool peach wood, to seal the deal right there.

Harwin slid off his overcoat with the aid of the mustard-eyed butler and then raised his hands. The great entrance hall with the marble floor, the baroquely papered walls bedecked with a gallery of governors past, and the deep crimson carpet leading toward the grand staircase was like a great echo chamber. As the governor and his brother watched, Harwin's shoulders trembled and the wave of sensations rolled across his muscle, into the wood, and down to the tips where the fingers of the beech and peach hands slowly spread out like fiddlehead ferns in the rain. The antennae spread, Harwin began to walk slowly about the hall.

"This presence," the governor began, "has been with us since we moved in."

"Before, even," the brother added, then coughed out, "I mean, perhaps."

"We need you to find it," the governor said. "Find it and contain it."

"And then?" Harwin asked.

The brother groaned. "And then you just leave that to us, boy."

As Harwin went, his arms trembled, shaking like branches in a breeze, although nothing was blowing in that big stuffy house. Harwin checked the hallways and the sitting rooms; the grand stairs and the narrow servants' steps in back; the kitchen, the bedrooms, and the privy, too, his fine and fancy arms out before him, testing the air, and the governor and his brother lumbering behind. He even checked in the basement with the cold black candles and the broken salt circle, although that too was empty, and the brothers shooed him out quick. All through the house, however, he could feel the tickle of something lurking just under the surface like a barn rat that got beneath a pie crust.

Everywhere he went in the mansion, Harwin felt the haint's threads, like when you step through a spiderweb and can't brush away the sticky feeling. He kept walking, spinning, doing the stations with no result, and all the while the two brothers dogged him to harumph and haw. The governor stood so close that he might as well have been a cape on the boy's shoulders, while the brother hobbled along on his bandaged foot, the two canes always tapping just behind, and the mustard-eyed butler lurked in the shadows. Harwin searched every nook and every corner, but although the sense of a presence never left, the gentle tug it exerted on the fine and fancy arms was always like the river's current on a fishing line—never the trout's bite.

The sun was rising, and the big blanks of the drawing room windows were starting to light, when Harwin, bone-tired and weary from hours on edge, had to surrender. He turned to face the brothers, head hung in disappointment both at his failure and at the prospect of losing the absurd purse he'd been promised. Then the trout bit.

Harwin staggered forward as the arms wrenched him toward the governor's brother. The man recoiled, but between the swollen foot and the rest of his ailments, he couldn't move far or fast. Luckily, Harwin locked his knees like a mule and leaned back, the straps and buckles holding his wonderful arms groaning as the limbs groped toward the brother. Whatever presence they had picked up on must have been missed at the first meeting in the foyer, but hours together had strengthened the call.

"Calm yourself," the brother bellowed as he swung one of his silver-handled canes at Harwin, clacking it against the straining arms.

"I'm sorry, sir," Harwin grunted against the strain of keeping them away. "They seem to be pulling toward your, err, foot."

In short order, and despite the very profane protestations, the governor and the mustard-eyed butler got the brother up onto the billiards table, pinned him down by the arms, and peeled the soiled bandages away from his foot. The appendage was enormously engorged and horrendously gouty, the big toe knuckle's tophus swollen like a mouse hiding beneath the tight red skin and all the rest of his little piggies swelled up in crimson sympathy. The brother howled, "Don't you touch me!" but the governor gave Harwin a look to remind him just whose mansion he was in. Harwin nodded and let go of his efforts to control the arms.

Down the beech wood arm swung and cracked the brother right on the enormous ball of the gout, splitting the skin and bursting it like an egg. The brother screeched and fell backward, eyes rolled up in his skull by the pain as the beech wood fingers pinched and dug into the chalky, white discharge. Even Harwin had to turn away as they rooted, but then they clacked shut, and he began to pull. Slowly, surely, inch by inch, Harwin prised the haint out of the mess left of the big toe knuckle. It stretched out like dough, the ghastly face of it elongating as Harwin pulled, but then it snapped and Harwin fell back, ankles over wooden elbows, the haint in his hands. It squirmed and cussed, but Harwin held it tight.

"Get me a box or a jar!" Harwin shouted from where he sat sprawled on the floor. "Something made of maple or iron or glass. Quick!"

The governor and the mustard-eyed butler hurried out of the room, leaving the brother splayed out on the billiard table's felt and Harwin clutching the haint in his fine and fancy hands. The brother moaned from where he lay, insensate from the agony of his flayed gouty toe.

"Hey, you," the haint said, the voice high and growly from between Harwin's clasped fingers. Harwin peered in. It looked like a little man in a suit, with a goat's head but with three long horns. It stared directly at him. "Let's talk."

A half-hour later, Harwin left the Governor's Mansion with a sack of money and another little tin pin bearing the State Seal. The governor had taken his brother, only just back from the bliss of unconsciousness, to his room to await a doctor. The brothers took with them a Mason jar, sealed with red wax, and wrapped in butcher paper with the Lord's Prayer written on it which Harwin swore to them would keep the haint contained so long as they never opened it to check. Only the yellow-eyed butler—still in his coattails—saw Harwin back outside and into the long black car.

When Great-Uncle Harwin got out of that long black car, he was rich by Mosby County standards. In just shy of a year, however, he was rich by any standards. His talent for witching out the lost, and now the damned as well, had always been strong, but now his success was absolutely prodigious. Lost rings were found buried in boxes of stolen jewelry which, unclaimed, went to Harwin. Just walking to the general store, he couldn't help but trip over a roll of paper money. He even found a small vein of emeralds once while planting tomatoes in his garden.

And what about the other kind of work? Ever since the story spread of Gaith Mathel and the pig witched out by Harwin, people had begged him to plumb out their haints and horribles. Harwin had turned them all down at his father's wishes, but, by coincidence, his father passed away shortly after he returned from the Governor's Mansion. Again—Mosby County, a hard life of sharecropping—there's no reason to assume that Harwin's father's death involved foul play or spirits. None at all. Don't even ask.

In any event, after the appropriate period of mourning, Harwin had no reason to turn those jobs down. The work just kept coming.

Those midnight jobs, however, are stories best saved for a different time. There isn't a family still living in Mosby County—and more than a few who aren't—that doesn't have a story about an uneasy spirit, ghost light, or other apparition which Harwin wrestled down and cast out with his fine and fancy arms. It will suffice to say he earned enough to buy the largest house in Mosby or even Statesville County, set on top of Mosby County's highest hill. It had one room for Harwin and his radiant wife, who he brought home from one trip out to the mountains for a particular witching and who kept mostly to herself; one for his frail mother, who had never quite recovered from the heart attack in the field; one for his baby son—Jesus save that boy, too—for that's a tragedy; and enough space left over still for the help and for Harwin to lose track of anything that wasn't strapped onto him.

For a time, too, witching took Mosby and Statesville and Degram and Dutch Counties like a craze. In those years, you couldn't find a tree with a Y-shaped branch left within the county lines if your life depended on it. A whole generation of Mosby County's children never learned to shoot a sling-shot, and although Grandma wouldn't say it, I think she believed that's why they lost so many boys in the war. Harwin himself, of course, made no small amount of money selling and signing such implements, although his own luck never seemed to rub off.

No, Harwin's new source of luck seemed to reside entirely within those fine and fancy arms. He was never seen without them, and although he never talked about it, gossip spread that ever since that night at the Governor's Mansion, he had something extra in those arms.

Ham Stetelson once said he saw the arms—by themselves, no Harwin—out by the mash still, dancing and pouring tumblers of moonshine over one another, but then Ham would get real quiet when you asked him where this still was. Winnie Jeffs said she saw them walking along the road one moonlit night, crawling on their fingers like spiders with the arms up in the air like meaty tails, but why she was on the road at night, she wouldn't say. Still, the whispers were eventually enough that they got out of Mosby County—Dutch County, too—and must have even made it back to the Governor's Mansion.

It's no secret that in the intervening years the state had fallen into tough times. The whole country had, it seemed, but avid readers of the local rags would have known that, on the whole, the governor and his brother had done far worse. Just for instance, the brother's position as a chair of the agricultural department had been cut; several of their joint investments came under heavy scrutiny; and one very unfortunate stable fire had killed five prized thoroughbreds, three and a half of them belonging to the governor. It was, perhaps, no surprise then, when Harwin received a hand-delivered message in a stiff white envelope dropped off by a long black car.

"Give it back."

Harwin's little boy's nanny saw it before Harwin tore it up, and that's all she said it said.

Now, I can only speculate—and Grandma would have had my hide for it, being just one step up from gossip—but I believe the letter was from the governor and his brother. I believe they had deduced, or at least they believed they had deduced, that Harwin had taken the haint that night and secreted it away inside his fine and fancy arms. They would, of course, have been too careful to say so in a letter, but I believe they had long ago brought the haint from the Just Beyond Here to help them accumulate their wealth, and one night it had gotten away from them, hiding first in Governor Ledsome's brother's gouty toe until Harwin had extracted it and then smuggled it out beneath their noses in his beech and peach wood arms. I also believe the governor and his brother were too subtle to send a hatchet man with a literal ax to extract it from Harwin, because whether for decorum or demonology, I think they wanted the transfer to be willing. They'd invited Harwin into their house to find the haint—and he had—and now it was Harwin's until he chose to hand it over.

Of course, that could just be me rationalizing things, as is my wont.

Whatever the reason, Mosby County began to suffer peculiarly under the governor's attention. A series of draconian regulations applying only to a very specific subset of farms raised taxes by 300% in one year. A local tobacco surcharge bottomed out prices the next. On the third, a state of emergency was declared with respect to the South American cotton weevil which, of course, had only been reported in Mosby County, resulting in the cull of the entire crop. The rates for the tenant farmers rose and evictions followed. Landowners signed off with shadowy consortiums whose "development plan" was to let the fields lay fallow until such time as they changed their minds. All of the schools were closed, the hospital in the next county shuttered, too, and somehow even the Church of the French Jesus lost its tax-exempt status with the state.

Through it all, though, Great-Uncle Harwin, high on the hill, prospered. People hired him to find their lost family plots now, looking for any burial goods their kin may have had. He was brought to even the barest clapboard shack to search for hidden treasure. Everyone had a haint they thought was killing their animals or poisoning their wells, though maybe the governor had men for that too? The witching craze hit a fever peak, and although no one would risk offending Jesus by asking Harwin to bless their rods, they'd still offer him a handful of dimes just to touch them and say, "Good luck."

This was the time, too, when everyone who had even a quarter—never mind a half—of a talent for witching started eyeing Harwin's arms, wondering if they, too, might better amplify their aptitude through certain judicious replacements. This, I have determined, is when Waller's Holler— home of the fabled lost Confederate gold—became known as Stump's Hollow. I won't elaborate on the obvious reason.

At this point, Harwin withdrew into his fine and fancy house, with his fine and fancy arms. His wife was pretty and fancy, his baby healthy and fine, but there on that highest hill, he could watch Mosby County around him dying. The governor's grip of taxation and regulation choked it off until the fields were brown. The well-off folks fled, leaving big empty houses with broken windows. Those too poor to go had given him the last of their cigar box savings from under the floorboard in the hopes he might find a forgotten haul or something dropped by chance. The line of half-armed men and children left a trail of blood from Stump's Hollow, up the hill, to his front door, all hoping for just a touch of his fine and fancy luck so that they, too, could strike it just rich enough to survive.

What must it have been like, I ask you now, to have been Great-Uncle Harwin, surveying the landscape you'd helped create? To know, too, that out of all of this ruin, you—by the luck alone of what was in your arms—would be fine? Would you have given it up willingly? Would you have unstrapped those arms of beech and peach and put them in a box and handed them to the driver of a long black car? Would you have given up your house on the high hill in the hopes the fields would grow again and Judd Brumb, Ham Stetelson, and the Lewis family with their Polish chickens might all come back?

Or might you have tried to hold on, with your fine and fancy arms? Might you have tried to prepare your baby boy for that fallow world out beyond your windows where the only way to live was witching? What would it have taken, I wonder, for Harwin to press his baby boy's rosy arm still beneath his cool, beech palm? Would he have thought it was a kindness to prepare him for that world while still so young? Could Harwin have asked his wife to wrap his peach wood fingers around a meat cleaver's grip and told the nanny to get the towels ready? Could you?

But, Mosby County, even the son of a rich water witch—there's no reason to assume Harwin's baby boy's passing involved foul play. Whooping cough, croup, cholera, consumption, feral pigs. A baby boy could die on any day ending in Y, especially with the nearest hospital shuttered.

Regardless of how, when it happened, Harwin broke. His wife and his help disappeared that very evening and the curtains were drawn and even the folks down in Stump's Hollow said you could hear the wailing rolling down from the house on the hill. It was only Winnie Jeffs, walking down the road in the early morning—coming home from where, she would not say—who saw Harwin standing at the end of his drive, handing an oblong box to someone in the back of a long black car. He was wearing the old welfare-issue arm prosthetics he had first been given as a boy, although now two sizes too small, but still with rough leather cuffs and rusty hooks. And that was that—the end of Harwin's witching.

There isn't much left to tell. Harwin sold the big house and moved himself and his mother to the bottom of the hill, into the tiny house where he remained for the rest of his days. The rest of the money he'd saved, and all but a pittance of what he earned through the rest of his life, he split amongst the Mount Zion, First Free Will, and Free First Will Baptists to distribute as charity. Over the years, Harwin and Mosby County survived, although neither ever fully recovered. Whatever happened to Governor Ledsome, or his brother, or the fine and fancy arms—well, let us say that they died. And let us say it was in some horrible way that would make us all feel better, even if I don't know that that's true.

And as to whether anyone else in my family has the witching, I cannot say. I can tell you only that I sit here before a sheet of paper, wooden pencil in my hand, letting it tell its lies and scratch out truths of its own accord, in the hopes that we might yet find a sense of meaning, or at least what passes for it in the end.

Paper Wings and Arrow Juice

This afternoon, after I finished talking with Justin, I found a very peculiar little fella. It's been all I could think about, and even at this evening's services I could hardly focus on what the pastor was saying given how my mind kept—well, hold on. The point of this journal is to keep things clear and help me remember them right, so I'll try to tell it as straight as I can.

I woke up this morning at the usual time and made myself toast. Thinking back on it, there was something a little different on the air. A sweetness, maybe, but heavier than just the guest soap in the bathroom or the bowl of dried potpourri in the spare room. It's funny, isn't it, how you don't think of those things at the time, but all the azaleas and the dogwoods are in bloom now, so I must have just thought it was the flowers. Oh, Harriet, this is why you're keeping the journal—to be more grounded and less forgetful.

Lordy, this is hard. I just want to skip to the thing I found, but I shouldn't, should I?

I did some cleaning, watched some television. For lunch I had a small salad and some canned salmon (low mercury). After that I called Justin. He was working from home, so I got to talk to him for a while, and although I did most of the talking it's just nice to hear his voice sometimes. When I asked if he was seeing anyone now, he was very...well, noncommittal. My poor grandson. *It must be so hard finding someone these days that I just don't even know how one even begins.*

That's not why I'm not seeing anyone, of course. Dear George will always be my true love, so while I want the best for Justin (and everyone else, really), I just don't have any more desire myself to be coupled off. I'm really not lonely at all.

Mercy me, I didn't mean it to sound like that. Anyway, after I hung up with Justin is when I found it—the cupid. I had just settled back in at the television when I heard a sound like death. It took me a moment to realize it was Larry yowling and spitting from the front room, but by the time I got there he was hiding beneath the good sofa and whatever he'd been at was fluttering and flapping on the ground.

At first, I thought it was a bird, but the wings—what was left of them—weren't right. They were tattered, but not like Larry or another cat had been at them. Or, not just that a cat had been at them. They looked like—like newspaper fluttering, maybe, or a giant moth with its powdery wings all crumpled and torn. It was a ratty pigeon, I thought, blown in from outside. A broken version of something you see every day. It must be.

But then I got closer—slowly, of course. You can never be too cautious. And, boy, what a sight.

The body of it wasn't any bigger than my thumb and Larry had done a number on it, but it was a cupid. Cross my heart and on the Lord, that's what it was. A little man, pink and scraped to dickens, but it had all its little dolly limbs and those paper wings, even a teeny winky that I only saw because he was naked as a jaybird. And his lips, I remember thinking, were like a tiny little bow—all red and arched, pursed together and stuck out almost like a beak.

The cupid looked at me as I drew up to it. Like little jewels, his eyes flashed up at me, and he scrambled toward a tiny little thing on the floor that I first thought was one of my knitting needles. But that poor thing, with its arms and legs scraped down by cat's teeth, slipping in the blood and it wings soaking it up and still fluttering to beat the angels.

The cupid died there next to the rug. Not on it, though, so I didn't have to get the cleaner.

Speaking of angels, that's how I knew it wasn't an angel. Well, first off, because angels don't die. Second, they don't have winkies or other downstairs parts. But also, the thing the cupid was reaching for as it died and I thought was a knitting needle? It must have been sharper than I thought, because I picked it up with a tissue but it tore right through the paper and one sharp end just barely grazed me. Just the tip, mind you, but oh Lord, the love I felt that night!

All the way to church with the Johnstons—bless their hearts for driving me this week—I felt a bliss surrounding me from all sides, coming at me from the left and right and up from under the car seat. The air sounded brighter and the colors of the trees and blossoms in the evening sunset tasted wild. I thought about borrowing someone's cellular phone to call Justin, but when we got to church and I saw the crucifix as you enter the chapel, I was overwhelmed by the shiny body of Christ. I thought—thought—it was the love of Jesus coming through the moist air and washing me away, but as we sat there, I began to realize it was something else.

As I watched Pastor Jim move around during the sermon, his crew cut and his strong shoulders bobbing... Well, I'm an old woman and I have modesty, but I still remember what it feels like there—you know where—when there's a more earthly kind of love getting worked up. That's how I know that it was a cupid that pricked me, not an angel. And with that, I am beat and will go to bed.

———

Even though Justin only lived ninety minutes away from his grandmother, it could feel like a different state. His glass nook of an apartment downtown was the opposite of the home he'd grown up in after his parents passed and where she still lived. Here, he was high above the ground and hemmed in by neighbors, buildings, street-level retail, and restaurants. Here, it was always alive with the bustle that had seemed impossible just a dozen or so years ago when he was an out-of-place teen in eastern farm country. Any illusion of true distance, however, dispersed on those spring days when the azaleas in the building's common areas bloomed and the dogwoods reaching out from their planters in the pedestrian malls threw open their tissue-thin blossoms. Despite sometimes feeling so far removed from that life, he was still only ninety minutes away—it would be half that when the bypass went in—and, he had been reminded almost an hour ago when his grandmother's number peaked out from his Caller ID, not even really that.

"Yes, Granma," he said into the phone. From the kitchen table, his laptop gaped at him, its cursor blinking from a half-composed email that had sat cooling since the phone rang. "Mmmhmm." He watched his hand crawling almost of its own accord, spinning webs of doodles in the margins of stale printouts. "Yes, but I need to— Right. Mmmhmmm."

From across the open layout living room-cum-dining area, a key clicked in the front door. Shoulder first, Justin's boyfriend, Tyler, wedged his way into the apartment, canvas bags of groceries dangling from his hands and the unruly leaves of the day's mail clasped beneath one elbow like a broken wing. He struggled as the straps of one overstuffed bag clutched at the door-knob and pulled him out of balance. As he muttered and tugged at the bag, his sunglasses slid down the bridge of his nose and he cursed as he craned his head back to right them, finally catching sight of Justin at the table.

"Could you just—" Tyler began, but Justin cut him off with a sharp look and pointed to the phone. *Shhh*, he pantomimed.

"I have to go, Granma," Justin said, rising from his seat. He made his way to Tyler, protesting as he did: "Really, Granma, I'm fine. I'm not lonely, but I have to— Yes, but I have to go now, really. Okay, okay. Love you too. Bye."

Justin reached Tyler just as he ended the call, but Tyler, now freed, pushed by. "Don't bother," he said, ignoring Justin's open hand.

Behind the granite island that separated the kitchen area from the rest of the main room, Tyler set about putting the food away. Vegetables went in the refrigerator, grains in the cabinets, wine in the racks. Justin, unwilling to watch Tyler brood, thumbed through the stack of today's envelopes. It was nothing good, of course.

"It was my Granma," he finally said. "You know how she is."

Tyler had put away the last of the cleaning sprays under the sink and let the door sharply fall into place. He was silent for a moment, and then took off his sunglasses, the crease of his brow still darkening his eyes. "Does she know about us yet?"

Justin looked down at the mail. It was never anything good.

"I mean," he began, "you know how she is."

"Seriously?" Tyler tensed, and for a moment Justin expected him to erupt. He would throw his sunglasses onto the floor, or sweep one big arm across the counter and wipe everything away in a single violent motion. It was like a spring storm building up between them, the sky ready to fall.

But then it deflated, all the electricity leeching from the air without even a spark. Tyler turned and walked from the room.

"I told her," Justin called out. "I just think, you know, some people only hear what they want."

———

"A foolish consistency is a hobgoblin," I think is how the saying goes. Anyway, it seems to me that it's foolish to run through every uneventful minute of the day when such exciting things are happening.

Do you remember my cupid? (That's not a serious question, I know this is a journal and will not answer me.) Well, today I found more! That's right, today I found two of them, just crawling around the edges of the breadbox. I think they were sniffing at the sugar cake inside, but when I came into the kitchen and saw them, I knew this was a sign. They were so set to their snuffling and licking at the sweetness around the edges that I managed to get them under a Pyrex with no problem.

They looked a little put out at being under there, sure, but not angry. The two of them kept smooshing their little faces against the baking glass and they looked so sorrowful that I put a soda cap full of Mountain Dew under there for them. Oh boy did they go wild for that!

I left them alone for just a bit to go to the bathroom and then tried calling

Justin, but he didn't answer. When I got back to the kitchen, though, they'd guzzled themselves into a bloated sleep and I noticed that they had dropped a little pile of those needle-shaped things. After the effect that last one had on me—and I still feel a little flushed when I look back on those pages I wrote while afflicted—I knew that these were the cupids' arrows, but I didn't know how they worked.

Carefully, so carefully, I tipped the Pyrex up and, using my gardening gloves, picked up the arrows. With the help of my reading glasses, I could see they were more like feather quills that were not solid, but sort of like a hollow tube. Little silver strings of liquid stretched from the tip of an arrow wherever it touched anything—my gloves, the table, the tissues when I tried to wipe it away. I didn't dare test them for sharpness after the last time, but I could see that there was more of that stuff inside them.

I've seen more than enough television with daytime doctors to know how science works, so I came up with a test. To start, I took the Mr. Whiskers treats from the cupboard—and, boy, was Larry already in the kitchen as soon as he heard that box rattle—and I broke one of the arrows over it. A smell like fabric softener filled my nose, but I squeezed the arrow and let the drops of that, well, love juice, I guess, drip out onto one of the treats.

I didn't know if Larry would eat it, but he did. Not only did he eat it, but he went wild! I haven't heard him yowl like that since before he was fixed, and even so he was going simply crazy, having his way with pillows, arm rests, the scratch post, everything. Finally, I just opened the kitchen door and he tore out back, sniffing the air and tail bolt-straight like that old cartoon skunk.

Well, I thought, that proves it. As Larry streaked out to relive his pre-neuter days, all I could think was that now I have a way to help bring people together. Especially Justin. My poor lonely boy. It must be so hard for him to find a good man. Anyone but that awful Tyler, really.

———

The restaurant Justin had picked occupied the same space as the Thai bistro he and Tyler had frequented the first time they were dating, but things moved so quickly that over the course of the cheating, the breakup, their life apart, and their recent reunion, the place had changed into some kind of New American deal. Still, he hoped the place held some lingering sentimentality even if the original faux-bamboo interior had been stripped out and reupholstered in plush darkness. He had chosen a public place because it was obvious Tyler would not enjoy the evening's conversation, but the risk of him breaking something dramatically decreased when they were not at home. It was during the appetizer course, as he listlessly forked at his honey-roasted Brussels sprouts and watched Tyler tear into his rabbit rillettes, that Justin broached the subject of his grandmother.

"I'm worried about her," he began. Tyler merely grunted as he smeared a forkful of meat in the rich sauce on his plate.

"When I talk to her," Justin continued, "she sounds more and more..." The words wouldn't come—not ones that he could risk saying out loud and summoning into reality.

"She is pretty old," Tyler said. His plate cleared, his eyes turned to Justin's starter. Despite his annoyance at Tyler's bluntness, watching him wiggle his dark brows in comic silence to beg for just one morsel, Justin couldn't help but smile. Justin raised his hands in surrender and slid the plate forward. Perhaps a full Tyler would be a happy Tyler.

It wasn't until their entrees arrived that Justin's grandmother re-entered the conversation. Although it would be difficult or expensive, likely both, Justin proposed moving her to a home, one nearer to if not *in* the city. God bless her neighbors who, out of Christian charity, took her shopping and to church, but it didn't seem safe for her to be living alone. Justin braced for Tyler's response, but whatever sympathetic magic was still in the walls of the restaurant must have worked, because Tyler didn't yell or slam his fist or even give Justin *The Glare*. Instead, he ground his mouthful of filet for a moment, swallowed, and then very calmly spoke.

"Did she ask for this?"

"No," Justin replied. "I haven't even asked her yet."

"Then you should let her stay."

"But I'm worried," Justin said. Tyler hadn't spoken to her, so he wasn't aware of how loose her grasp on things seemed to be getting. He didn't see how, although their conversations were on the same topics as ever—that week's sermon, who had died, who was courting, when was Justin going to find someone and settle down—the whole tenor had changed. It was as if there was something too involved under her questions; there was another layer that surfaced as an uncommon intensity and inability to focus.

"She won't even want to come," Tyler said. "So let's leave her be." A forkful of steak crammed into his mouth indicated it was closed to further discussion, but Justin wasn't done.

"Why do you hate her so much?"

"Because she hates me!" The juices sprayed from around Tyler's clenched teeth in the angry hiss. Justin felt the eyes of the nearest tables on them, but Tyler was oblivious. He seethed, and the tealight candles flickered as the restaurant's magic began to crack under his barely restrained anger.

"She's always hated me. Ever since we started dating, even before I—" He bit back the words he was going to say. "Even before anything happened, she's always had it out for me."

"That's not true," Justin said, although he couldn't remember if it was or not.

"Of course it is." Tyler curled his lips and shook his head, the way he did whenever Justin ought to know or do something, but was too stupid or weak. "She wouldn't even stop trying to set you up while we were together. I was never good enough for her sweet baby boy."

The room was hot and all the wine in Justin's stomach was turning old bruises into deep red pools. "Maybe you weren't," he said.

Tyler snorted. "That's her talking, not you. I love you, but you are such a granny's boy." Taking his napkin from his lap, he wiped his hands and threw it over the half-eaten meat like a shroud.

———

I'm trying to reinstate a structure on these entries because I feel like I may have gotten distracted. The diary form wasn't helpful, but also I don't want to lose track of my important discoveries, since I feel a little all over the place these days. When I start helping people, it's going to be very important to keep things in order. In that spirit...

First, I found what I think is the cupids' nest. Well, no, I know it is. It's just, writing it down makes it different, doesn't it? But it's in the spare room. It looks like a wasp nest, mostly, but larger since the cupids are so much bigger. You can still see the gray and white print where they chewed up and spit out my newspapers to make it. It's clear that's what they've been using because the stacks of The Observer *I've been collecting have all these little Swiss cheese holes in them and I've seen those little cupids crawling over it, cheeks red as cherries, just working it like chaw and plopping it on bit by bit. The main part of their nest hanging from the ceiling corner is the size of a laundry basket, but there's another smaller section that looks fairly new sort of stuck on the side of it. That part's the size of a small dog, maybe.*

I'm keeping the door to the spare room closed from now on, but dealing with that can wait because...

The arrows work on people! After I'd found the nest in the spare room (How could it have been growing there so long? This is what you get for neglecting your hospitality, Harriet, even though the house smells like there are dried flowers in all the walls), after I found it, I couldn't help but notice the piles of little arrows littered on the floor around it like droppings. Well, that doesn't make it sound appetizing, but nevertheless I got my gardening gloves and scooped them up.

It's late and I'm tired so I'll skip the nitty-gritty, but after a rather trying talk with Justin this afternoon, I was in a sort. Luckily, I told him I'd pray on our disagreement, and I was fortunate enough for it to be Miss Sarah who gave me a ride to church tonight. It's shocking to me that she's all alone, given that she's still fairly young and has that pretty yellow hair, but during the service I couldn't help but notice she was making eyes at the Stilts' oldest boy, Henry. He's a tall, sturdy one and that got me thinking, so while we were saying our goodbyes after the service, I asked if he wouldn't mind coming back with us to change a light for me. He hesitated, but I might have acted a little frailer than I really am and Sarah, bless her heart, said she'd drive him home after. It wasn't a lie, of course, because I really do have a light in the spare room that needs changing. Anyway, neither of them seemed to overly mind the other's company as we rode back.

Although when we got home I'd have described them as "friendly" at best, I've made enough matches in my time to spot a real connection. I told Henry about the light in the spare room, but before he got to it, I offered them both a glass of iced tea with some of that arrow juice in it. Well, I don't want to be crude, but there was a tension in the air. Even I felt hot and bothered just watching from the side.

I excused myself, saying I had to go outside and look for Larry since his food hadn't been touched yet. Standing out there in the warm evening, the smell of honeysuckle hanging low on the ground, I called quietly to Larry, not wanting to disturb anything that might be going on inside. Oh, to be young and on the verge of that dangerous thing called love once more.

Anyway, I was out there for a while without finding Larry, although I'm not worried—he is a cat after all. When I went back in, though, there wasn't a trace of Henry or Sarah other than their half-drunk tea glasses sweating on the table. The bulb I'd left for Henry to put in was still there too.

They hadn't left out the back door or they would have passed me, and Sarah's car is still here, but I'm not worried. They're young and in love, after all. They probably went out the other side to take a walk under the stars. I'd thought to wait up for them, writing this entry as I do, but now that I'm done, it's well past my bedtime. Good for them though. They're the first of many lonely people I can help now that I know the arrows work, so let them enjoy it.

I'll call Justin tomorrow and let him know that I'm ready to help solve things between him and Tyler.

———

He told her that he was with Tyler again. She told him she could find him someone better. He told her again that he was with Tyler and that wasn't going to change. She told him that if he just came to visit her, she could find him someone irresistible. He told her that he and Tyler were together and that if she couldn't respect his choice, he wasn't sure that these calls should continue. That stopped her.

"I have to go," she said. "Sarah is coming to get me for church, but I'll pray on it."

They exchanged their I love yous and goodbyes.

Would that be it? Justin didn't have much faith in prayer, but despite his doubts, his grandmother called back the next day, eager to make amends. She only wanted to see him happy, of course, and although she wouldn't ever forget what Tyler had done, she could try to forgive him for Justin's sake. In fact, she wanted to do everything in her power to make things right.

Justin cried. His grandmother cried. Tyler snorted but held his tongue and, with some coaxing, agreed to drive down for dinner—only dinner—that weekend. Justin's grandmother said "Hallelujah" and that she would whip up something special, just for them.

That Saturday evening, as they pulled around in back of Justin's grandmother's house, cicadas and crickets were going wild in the amber light. A million singing insects swam in the muggy air and seas of grass around them, the chatter of their music making the air tremble like syrup. Another car was already parked around back, but Justin didn't recognize it. He hoped that this wasn't a set-up, that his grandmother hadn't secretly invited another suitor, but if Tyler shared the same concern, he hid it well. He merely dabbed at the beads of perspiration already crawling from his hairline as they left the air-conditioned car and headed up to the screened-in back porch.

"I want you to behave," Justin whispered as he knocked on the door. "Whatever happens."

"Trust me, by the end of the night, she's going to want to kiss me," Tyler said. "They don't call me Mr. Charming for nothing."

"They don't call you Mr. Charming at all." Justin knocked again and turned the knob. The door was unlocked, but his grandmother was one of those good country people who couldn't believe a neighbor would do her wrong. Out here, there was nothing but the neighbors and the bugs in the field.

"Granma," he called out as they entered the kitchen. The ceiling fan spun slowly above various dinner items that remained half-made—breaded but not fried chicken; okra that was washed but not cut. A pair of gardening gloves sat like empty skins beside the sink. A pool of batter resting in a cake tray quivered beneath the oven light's red eye.

"Granma?" Justin called again. The house's single bathroom just off of this room was open and empty.

"She's probably just up front," Tyler said. His eyes roamed over the unmade food, but finding nothing ready to eat, he opened the refrigerator and began to rummage through.

The house was a simple thing, barely one step up from a shotgun shack. From the kitchen, Justin could see through the open doors into the adjacent living room and the sitting room beyond. Their emptiness stared back at him. That left only his grandmother's bedroom and the spare room where she might be.

"Do you want some?" Tyler asked, pulling out a plastic jug filled to the brim with iced tea. Justin shook his head, so Tyler sloshed out the thick liquid into a single jelly jar glass on the counter. He took a sip. "Ugh." He shivered as he spoke. "I know you all love this stuff, but I don't see how you can drink it this sweet." He licked his lips, however, and then smiled wide and bright, baring his teeth. He raised it to his lips again.

"Could you go check the bedroom and the spare room up front?" Justin asked as he tried to swallow his panic. Tyler grunted and strolled out of the kitchen, still sipping from his glass.

Justin looked for any signs of where his grandmother might have gone. There were no notes on the refrigerator; nothing by the phone. She might have run out, but it wasn't like her to leave food uncovered and the oven on. If only he could find a number for that Sarah girl that took her to church maybe, or the Stilts family. Stiltsons? Something like that.

The shatter of glass rang through the house, and before he realized it,

Justin was barreling toward the front. The spare room was open and when he threw himself through the darkened doorway, he gasped.

Just inside the unlit room, Tyler stood like a dressmaker's dummy. The jelly jar's shards glittered in the remnants of tea, catching the wedge of light from the other room and casting it over a swarm of things like Justin had never seen. Already lapping at the puddle, they crawled and fell over each other, wings rustling like a thousand sheets of yellowed paper. Insects, he thought, bloated wasps or ants or something else awful. Then, between the tangles of their little arms and legs, he saw their smiling faces and pursed little lips.

Justin screamed. He grabbed at Tyler's arm to pull him away from the little creatures that were already licking the drops from Tyler's shoes and clutching at his pants cuffs. Tyler was a statue, though, his eyes fixed on a pulsating bulk in the deeper gloom.

A wasp's nest the size of a couch hung in the corner, its tattered gray shell throbbing as streams of the little creatures crawled from the chutes and cells. They shook their thick limbs and rattled their wings as they tumbled out and slapped onto the floor. Thick mud tubes spread from the central hive like crooked fingers daubed against the wall, shivering as the things scurried through them from other bulbous appendages.

In horror, Justin tried to take it all in, eyes growing wider to suck up enough of the paltry light to follow the tunnels. The next closest mass was a hive the size of a breadbox, but he recognized the four-legged outline and tufts of black fur sprouting from between its paper layers. Next to that, connected by the trembling tubes, was a massive knot of wax and daub that Justin could not untangle until he realized that the frayed golden strands through which the creatures crawled was a woman's hair. With that insight, the corpse's gnawed and pocked face came into focus through the shadows.

"Tyler!" He shouted to be heard over the madness of the crinkling wings and walls. He wrenched at Tyler's arm, but Tyler shoved him and, stumbling from the force, Justin fell over himself to the floor.

Lying prone, Justin watched his boyfriend walk across the field of glittering eyes, the things popping like Jerusalem crickets beneath his feet as each squelch made the air heavier and wetter with floral treacle. Crunching through the horde, Tyler made his way to the far corner, where Justin finally saw the other man.

The young stranger stood against the wall, his face placid but his body covered from the neck down as if he were sleeping upright in a newsprint bedroll. A heavy tube from the other clusters led beneath the shroud, tying the man back into the grim tapestry. With everything revealed to Justin, for a moment the creatures' rustling wings and the hives' trembling skin were waves on a distant shore. Justin watched himself watching Tyler sleepwalk over the sea of tea-drunk creatures, leaving great oozing holes behind him as he went toward the other man.

But then there was motion. The man's breast moved. Up, then down. A breath, Justin thought, scrabbling back into the moment and back upright. Another. Then another, but it was fast. It was too fast.

Justin stared as the rise and fall of the man's chest became an undulation, a wave that started in his belly and rolled up to his chest. The man's neck bulged, filling the loose skin, and his mouth opened as if to speak, but no sound came forth. Instead, it opened wide. Wider. Past the breaking point, it opened with a sound like tearing paper.

From inside that ragged hole beneath the stranger's dull, dead gaze, two new eyes peered out, pink like fresh buds. They twitched back and forth, taking in the nest, the swarm, Tyler, Justin. Liquid darkness shaped like claws trembled within and the broken jaw swayed.

Tyler leaned in close to kiss the quivering bow of the other man's lips.

———

I've had to start a new journal, but it's harder this time. The medicine, I think, might be making it difficult, but I'm going to try.

This place is nice. It's not my old home, and some of the other seniors here seem so sad, but it's closer to Justin and he comes by every weekend, so I don't much mind. I asked him when I can go back home, just to get a few things, and he keeps saying soon, soon, but it's already been...well, I'm not sure.

I guess this is what happens as you get older. It's funny, because I remember Justin and Tyler were coming to dinner and I had everything I needed except for enough sugar to make the cake icing. I called Sarah but she didn't answer—the Stilts either—and so I'd run out myself, thinking I'd just be a moment. I must have got turned around, though, I hate to say, and I was walking on the side of the road when I saw Justin's car. I waved to him and he pulled over and then things got very stressful.

Is it my memory? Medicine? Just old age? It's all in bits from there. Justin got me into his car. There was yelling, and he was driving fast. I remember being in a hospital bed, I think, with a handsome young doctor I couldn't help but notice didn't have a wedding ring. Now, here I am.

I'm getting tired—must be the medicine—so I'll wrap it up for today. I'll just say that I'm glad to rest a spell and be around other people for a bit. I wonder if any of them have any grandsons that Justin might like? I think he's single again.

Oh, and before I forget, I found one of those arrows in the pockets of the dress I was wearing that day Justin found me. But guess what? They aren't arrows at all! They're eggs, I guess, because one of them hatched and now I have another little cupid in a covered drinking glass beneath my bed. Soon, I'll be able to start helping people here, too, since I hate to see them so lonely.

A Song Like Laughter

Katrina had only just brought Bradley back inside and set him on the floor when a burst of hollow rapping shook the front door of their trailer. She wasn't expecting anyone—friends were scarce and her family hadn't visited since Bradley was born—and she hadn't heard the crunch of gravel in the driveway. Still, that didn't mean it wasn't Bradley's father, Joshua. He often dropped by unannounced and, sometimes, without his car if a bartender had taken his keys.

Bracing herself, Katrina picked up her heavy toddler and trudged beneath her burden toward the door. Even as she crossed the meager distance, another volley of knocking cracked against the thin door, and Bradley wailed. As she rocked him, Katrina stared at the broken tail of the chain lock that Joshua had shattered last month. Not for the first time, Katrina wished she'd gotten around to fixing things up.

"Who is it?" she called.

"It's me," replied a voice that rose and fell in singsong inflection. It sounded male, mostly, but the enunciation and the intonation vibrating through the thin particleboard were unfamiliar.

"Come on, darling," it sang again. "I don't have all day."

Katrina unlocked the door and slid it open just enough to peer through the crack, but there was no one waiting to meet her gaze. The yard and driveway were empty, too. She opened the door a little wider.

"Hey. Down here."

An enormous gray and white bird squatted on the steps. Its head reached her hips and, from the tip of its hooked black beak to the end of its flight feathers, it was almost as long as Katrina was tall. The snowy feathers on its breast burst against the thundercloud cowl of its head and wings.

"I thought you'd never answer," it said.

"Oh," was all Katrina could say. "Are you—Oh." Her knees wobbled and the world fluttered as her vision dimmed.

"Hey!" the bird said. "Be careful!"

The bird's sharp words embarrassed Katrina out of her shock. She rooted herself to the ground and held Bradley tighter.

"What are you?" Katrina asked. She stared at the bird. "What are you doing here?"

"You know why I'm here, my dear." The bird's voice sparkled, dark and sweet. "Our deal is done and now I've come."

"Come for what?"

The bird cocked his head and blinked his bright yellow eyelids. From her angle above, however, it looked to Katrina as if he was winking.

"My son, of course." And he sang like laughter.

———

As the bird sang, Katrina's mind flew away, just a little, and when it returned, she was seated in a lawn chair, watching as the giant bird hopped around the yard. With its thick talons, it furrowed the ground and then ran its scythe-like beak through the trenches. In Katrina's lap, Bradley strained against her arms, gurgling in wordless joy as the bird raked and pecked at the earth.

"I'm sorry," Katrina said, waking up to her surroundings. "But who are... Your son? Are you... Joshua?" She craned forward, looking for marks or scars that might reveal the man she knew—and sometimes loved—buried beneath the feathers.

The bird sang like laughter again. "No, no. Do you really not remember me?"

She shook her head.

"My name is," and he sang a trill that no human could replicate. "And we met back when, goodness, how old is he now?" *Trill* hopped toward them, pointing to Bradley with his beak.

"Bradley? He's two. Two-ish."

Trill stared. Katrina looked into his eyes but found only her own reflection in the storm-black sheen.

"He's big for his age," she said, unsure how to continue. She pinned Bradley's outstretched arms down and away from the bird's thick beak.

"Don't you wonder why that is?" *Trill* asked.

"His father—Joshua—he was big too."

"My dear," *Trill* said, his voice lilting into a melancholy air. "Do you really need me to tell you a story you already know?"

She nodded.

The bird exhaled sharply, almost like a sigh. Then he sang, and the notes of his words flocked around Katrina, nestling her into a warm, mosaic film.

———

I was flying past one evening, skimming over the trees and into the purple horizon, when I heard you crying. The song of your sorrow was so sad and so bitter that I would have cried, too, if only birds had tears. I felt like it was raining and even the Earth's magnetic fields were being washed away.

And so, I had to land.

And I circled down to perch in the tree outside your window—I was smaller then, you see—and I watched you sobbing.

And there was a man behind you who was screaming, squawking, and he circled you, pecking, looking for an opening.

And then he flew away and the door slammed shut behind him.

And you were by the window, framed in the light from inside. You put your hands on your stomach, and you cried and you cried.

And I knew then. I knew what I could do for you.

So, I came back the next evening. You were alone but you were still crying. The air was heavy with salt and the sound of glass inside your home was like a wind chime.

I knocked on the door and you opened it. And you were out-of-focus, your eyes blurred beyond tears, but when you saw me there with my egg, you said it was as big as the moon.

And the glow from the porch light lit it as you held it in your hands, no longer trembling. The luster spread up across your arms and face and eyes and body.

And you said, looking through me and through the shell and through the light, you said, "I used to have one of these."

And I nodded.

"He might love me," you said, "if I had another."

And I nodded.

And I folded you within my wings and I told you, I said, "You could have this one, but only for a while."

You nodded.

"But one day," I said, "one day, I will come back for him."

You nodded.

And you picked it up, my still-not-born son, and you walked back inside. I watched through the window, watched you sitting there, pressing the vessel into your lap. You were holding the shell, just like you're doing now.

———

Katrina found herself once again in the dark mirror of the bird's glossy eye. She didn't remember how she got there.

"I don't know," she said. "It sounds familiar, but it seems..." And she drifted off. As *Trill* had sung, the memories had built a nest around her; now that he had stopped, however, the stitches of her recollections were unraveling. But maybe, just maybe, it was like he said. Those had been such black days.

"And now, my dear," he spoke again, "I have to take him back."

"But you can't," she said. "You can't. I've kept him and I love him."

"And I thank you for that. But now it's time for me to take him. You can be free again."

"I don't think so. I don't know. I don't."

"Think of the open sky, the clear blue that awaits you."

"I don't want to be alone," Katrina whispered.

"But aren't you already?"

"But my son," Katrina said.

"My son," *Trill* sang.

The sky darkened between them as the sun dipped behind the tree line, spreading its shadow across the lawn like a great dark wing.

"You don't want this," he said, shuffling closer.

Bradley cooed and reached out his soft, pink fingers to rub the hard, black hook of *Trill's* beak.

Trill's breath rumbled softly as a new song, like some lullaby from a strange and distant country, crept from his tufted throat and wormed into Katrina's ears.

"You said it yourself, he's big for his age. But that's still albumen, and soon you'll see him change."

Katrina shook her head.

"Does he have all his teeth? No? That's because soon the points of his beak will protrude through his gums. And what you see now, these hen's teeth, will fall to the ground like snowflakes of bone."

Katrina pulled Bradley closer into her lap. *Trill* sang on, the images fluttering behind her eyes.

"You'll see it soon," he sang. "Soon, the pinfeathers will sprout from his back. He'll itch and he'll scratch; he'll cry and you'll cry. You'll pull at the tiny bits, digging at them like weeds. But the roots will come out in clumps. And they'll bleed and they'll bleed."

Katrina shook her head again.

"And he's heavy now, you said it, you did. He is. But soon his bones will be thin and hollow like paper, his fingers stretching back to his elbows and his shoulders locking into new forms."

Katrina started to cry.

"Has he started talking yet?" *Trill* went on, the air around Katrina roiling. "He won't, you know. Any day now, you'll hear him singing, to himself, like this," and *Trill* warbled. "It will be lovely. Until the next day or the next, when you stop finding it lovely. When his music has no words, not then and not ever."

Trill hopped and shook his feathers, the agitated rustling like bushes in a violent gale.

"And when the children, the neighbor children, and then the rest of the world begin to see how he is changing—whose son he really is—then they'll know." *Trill* croaked once. "Then they'll know what to do."

"What?" Katrina asked, bracing as if for a blow. "What will they do?"

"They'll take him. And cage him. Strip him. Pluck him. Scrape him. Open him up at the joints and—"

"Stop!" Katrina sobbed. "Stop."

Bradley had left her lap and was wiggling his way across the ground. The bird leaned over and nudged the boy with the curve of his beak. His scaled feet were large enough to carry Bradley, provided that *Trill* held him gently between his four toes. Seeing them so close together, Katrina couldn't detect the family resemblance, but children changed so much as they grew and she didn't even recognize much of herself, if any, in Bradley.

"They'll blame you," the bird said, lifting his wings as if to shrug. "They always blame the mother."

Katrina blinked again and again, but the images and lyrics from his story-song still drifted in her eyes.

"I—I know," she finally said. "I can't keep him, can I?"

"Nor do you want to," *Trill* said. He nuzzled her hand, clicking as he did. "But I need you to give him to me."

In a dream, Katrina walked over to where Bradley squirmed. She picked him up, kissed him quickly, then placed him down in front of the enormous bird.

"Can I go with you?" she asked, but she stared at the ground.

"No," *Trill* said. "I can't carry you both and you can't fly."

"Can't I just have a little longer?" She sank to her knees.

"No," *Trill* sang. "We have a long way to go and I'd rather not be late."

Katrina wept and tore at the grass. She clawed her nails through the dirt as *Trill's* talons and tail feathers bobbed across her field of vision. She watched the broken leaves rise beneath the beating of his wings and saw Bradley's feet leave the ground, straight up and out of sight. His squeal of joy echoed through the clearing, spiraling out in the wake of their ascension.

————

They left Katrina beneath them, dark and small in the dying day.

"Da-da?" Bradley said, reaching up to the talons that held him high in the evening sky.

"Sorry, kid," *Trill* said. "But I've never seen you guys before in my life."

And he sang as he flew, sang like laughter.

Junippy Paw

My first fiancé, Joe, possessed a brooding, old soul intensity that younger me found magnetic. A poet, a philosopher, an artist; he was my age, but his deep melancholy seemed a symptom of his special maturity and worldly insight. Who wouldn't have wanted to be wanted—to be needed, and at times desperately so—by someone like that? At least at twenty-two.

I'd breathlessly accepted Joe's late mother's ring as much for that reason as for the outsized heart I suspected he hid away, bruised by loss after loss. I could articulate it only later, but Joe was one of those men who defined himself by his sadness. It's understandable, isn't it, that I knew at some point that heart would finally break and that I wanted to be there for him when it did? I even thought maybe the time had come when his last living relative— a grandfather hidden off in the woods like a hermit—passed away shortly after our engagement.

Yet although Joe was overcome with such a profound moroseness that he left his grandfather's now-empty cabin to sit alone in the woods for over a year, we never quite reached that tipping point. While I still saw those dark, brilliant flashes of the Joe I'd fallen for—a painting or a poem he'd finish, the way he sometimes held me—they became rarer and harder to reach. I still was biding my time, however, until I could figure out a way to fix him. To fix it, I mean. What had been between us.

By process of elimination, we had always spent the holidays with my family, but by the second year of our long engagement and just about a year since his grandfather's death, Joe could clearly no longer stand being squeezed around the Thanksgiving table with my sisters, cousins, aunts, uncles, plus ones, and pets. He cowered behind the vivid bowls of pureed gourds and slipped away as soon as my back was turned. When my parents asked, I tried to laugh it off: "That's my fiancé—the ghost." As much as I'd wanted them to finally pay attention to their middle daughter when I'd accepted his proposal, it was embarrassing.

But while I told myself that we loved each other in our way, in intimacy and solitude, he was simply more withdrawn by nature than I was by nurture. Although I was his constant companion and he would say I was his world, would you understand me if I told you that I often felt alone?

We were incomplete in different ways, and while my initial infatuation had been born out of seemingly finding the one who could make me whole, over time I felt that we only filled each other's gaps. We slowly became just one person with just one functional life between us: we had one apartment, in his name; one car, in mine; and one set of acquaintances, which neither of us really wanted to claim. Shortly after that last dismal Thanksgiving, too, Joe decided we needed to move to a new city, away from my family, so that he could follow a job and, as a result, we had just his one income. He worked and I kept house: one life.

More and more, instead of a missing puzzle piece, I felt like a splinter of glass buried in a scar. I see now, of course, I was longing to work myself free, even as I held back for fear of the blood.

I was still grappling with this dawning sense of irreconcilability when I made the call and insisted that Joe and I spend the time between Christmas and New Year's finally attending to the disposition of his dead grandfather's cabin rather than putting on another show for my family. We were young, and even though I was telling myself that I couldn't feel us beginning to drift apart like ice floes, I wanted my love to be enough to fix it. If ever there was a time when I could save us, I thought that was it.

————

"What do you remember about your grandfather?" I asked as Joe drove. Joe hadn't ever mentioned him much, but he had been Joe's last living relative, at least until one abnormally cold and dark winter, after which, well, he wasn't. Given Joe's tendency toward morbidity, though, I didn't want to dwell on that, so I prompted him: "Tell me something good."

Joe didn't immediately answer, and for a moment I worried we might be in the doldrums of another silent spell, but then he began:

"In my memory," Joe said, "my father's sedan is grinding down the gravel of the driveway. Grandpa is standing on the porch and the sun is always just sinking behind the faraway mountains. In that light, the stream behind the cabin is a yellow ribbon where water bugs and hungry fish make little bullet hole ripples."

That word choice worried me, but I forced a smile. I reached across the console to touch him on the knee and his attention came back from where it was to the road before us.

"Tell me more," I said.

"Let's see," Joe said as I leaned back. "Well, one of Grandpa's hands grips the rail and the other is ruffling his silver hair as if he didn't remember we were coming and he's puffing himself up to fend off intruders. But then he recognizes Dad's car and waves." Joe paused. "And then he turns—Grandpa had this long nose, almost like a beak—and he whistles for Juniper, his Bernese mountain dog. She comes bounding out from the bushes, burrs and twigs tangled in her fur."

"What else?" I asked. "Tell me about your time together."

"Well," Joe hesitated. "If there's still light, we go fishing. Fish are hungriest right before the darkness sets."

"Mhmm." The car's heat was blasting, so I leaned against the cool window and let the motion rock me.

"Inside the cabin, everything is wood," Joe continued. "The floors, the ceilings, all the walls. And there's a cupboard door that was just my height, built into the wall that separates off Grandpa's bedroom, and that's where he keeps his outdoor gear.

"And inside, it's like bulrushes on a riverbank. Fishing rods of every size and type. And even though I only ever remember him using the same one, he makes this big production over which one to pull out, as if it's a life and death decision."

"And then?" I was nodding off, images of the cabin in the golden glow of Joe's youth lulling me toward sleep.

"Then he and I and Juniper head out into the dusk. We follow the stream down to the bend, just far enough that you can only see the cabin's roof. Here, he says, just in the crook with the deep wells and the branches of trees that wash down, this is where the big ones are hiding.

"So we take out the plastic margarine tub he's filled with night crawlers as thick as my pinky. And Grandpa pulls one out, wiggling, and sets the hook for me, and we cast our lines out into the deep water where the ripples grow."

Sleep was finally reaching up to take me. "What happens next?"

"Why does something have to happen?" he snapped, and the surge of his anger jerked me back. "Why can't it just be that?"

Although awake, I refused to look over and indulge him. He sighed dramatically.

"Then there's an accident," he said. "Juniper drowns just beyond the bend of the stream. Grandpa stops fishing. Pretty soon, Dad stops bringing me to visit. Dad dies. Grandpa dies. Now here we are."

I loved Joe, I swear, but at times there was just no talking to him.

———

It was a cabin in the woods, for all that dully functional description invokes. A blocky single story of tempered wood with a front porch and a peaked roof pierced by a woodstove's chimney pipe, it sat in a clearing at the end of a quarter-mile gravel driveway. The stream rolled by close enough that its whisper never ceased. I almost expected to see Joe's grandpa troubling his hair on the porch and Juniper bounding out from the back, but they weren't there, of course.

Joe had to fiddle with the lock a bit, but when we finally entered and he turned on the lights, I sighed. If not a romantic hideaway, I had secretly hoped for a thrilling ramshackle mess, but it was boringly tidy apart from the faint layer of dust and the one recently re-finished wall. I could still see where the timber had been scrubbed and the buckshot dug out. The wood filler compound had been spackled in and sanded down, but still didn't match the color or grain of the wood and daub of the other four walls.

Otherwise, nothing there hinted at any kind of disorder.

When I expressed surprise at how clean it was, Joe shrugged. I felt a twinge between pain and irritation when he told me he'd hired cleaners after the sheriff found Grandpa—special ones for the wall, of course, but who also put everything away and aired the house out. He certainly didn't need my permission, but why had this been the one thing he hadn't needed me for? It seemed silly to consider it a betrayal, but I couldn't help wondering what kind of other secret half-life Joe might be silently living in our single shared existence.

"It's nice," I said, taking pains not to use any of the tones he'd lately begun to find patronizing. "Maybe you could rent it out."

"I don't think so," he said. "Just look at this mess."

Other than the odd wall out, the open living room with its kitchenette and woodstove was accommodating, and the wide bare floor invited the company of tables and chairs. The doorway in the pockmarked wall leading back to the single bedroom and attached bath was still a mystery, but to me, the living room was a heart waiting to be hugged in carpets, given a splash of color, and brought back to life.

To Joe, unfortunately, the walls were a hedgerow maze from which he couldn't escape. The faded pictures and exposed book spines on the shelves that covered every wall except the damaged one were charms to me, but to him they must have been ticks and nettles. Still, I fancied I might help Joe by immunizing him to the memories drop by drop, as if they were a poison.

"Is this your grandfather?" I picked up a silver frame that held a black and white photograph of a couple. The man had a severe hawksbill nose and spidery fingers pressed against his chest as if making a pledge. The woman wore an ankle-length skirt, ruffled blouse, and a headscarf that cast everything but her brilliant teeth in a fuzz. The couple was young, but the picture was old, yet I recognized the cabin porch.

Joe turned from a shelf of leather-backed books. A stuffed owl above him was frozen in the middle of a hoot of dismay, rendered snowy by the dust. Joe just grunted in answer.

"I see the resemblance," I said. The words had come to me only for the want of something to say, but it was as if saying so had made it true and Joe's profile seemed sharper than I'd ever noticed before. For a split second, I could see him opening his mouth to acknowledge what I'd said and, instead of speaking, screeching like an eagle, but no. He was silent.

"I don't see Juniper," I said, trying to lure something else out.

"She didn't come until after she died," he snapped.

I bit my tongue, and then tried to smile. "A companion?" I asked.

He grunted. "A lifeline."

I shook my head, tired of tight lips and angst over every tiny thing. I didn't have time to fully ruminate, however, because then Joe spun like a compass needle brushed by a magnet. As if reeled in, he walked quickly toward the small cupboard built into the refinished wall and I followed, drawn equally by curiosity as by habit.

Up close, the rough spots of filler in the wall were as dull as plaster bandages. The cupboard door had been painted over and into its frame at one point, thick coats like a scab sealing it shut. It had been broken, though, and the cracks along the jambs stood out in the eggshell finish. Joe pulled the chest-high door's knob and, to my surprise, it opened eagerly and without a sound.

Inside was a canebrake of old fishing rods and broomsticks, the reedy pieces shrouded by fine cobwebs. I'd just as soon have junked them, but Joe seemed to hear a call from beyond those tools. He reached through the clustered shafts and gripped something in the back. He tilted it close enough to see—a double-barreled shotgun, still glistening with gun oil.

Joe frowned as he pulled it out. The twin barrels looked almost silver, marred only by a few bright orange scabs of corrosion. As I looked more closely, however, a pattern began to emerge. It wasn't the random pitter-pat of rain left to rust or the chaos of a splash. Instead, it was closer to a candle whose wick had been violently pinched and its small well of wax dripped down over the long steel fingers that had done it.

"Is that—" I caught myself. I knew it was, but it wasn't a topic I wanted to dredge up with my increasingly melancholy fiancé. Not while standing before the refinished wall which still bore the scars.

Joe bit his lip and held the weapon at arm's length. His hands had always been delicate, but they looked like a child's saddled beneath the iron of the gun, so I took it from him and opened the breech to check that it wasn't loaded. Safety assured, I examined the barrels. Despite the oxidation along the outside, which I didn't care to dwell on, the inside of the bores looked clean.

"Don't play with that," Joe pawed at the gun. "It's dangerous."

I twisted out of his reach. "It's safer with me."

Joe frowned. "What do you mean by that?"

I considered my words carefully. "My sisters and I were raised with guns," I chose to say. "Lizzie was a competitive shooter. You know that."

"Do I?" He shook his head.

"Don't you?" I replied.

Another discussion about secrets that weren't really secrets but only unasked questions loomed before us, but I flinched. I closed the shotgun and placed it next to the cabinet door as a show of good faith. Leaning there, it looked set to keep the fishing poles and lures in line, although I couldn't yet have imagined that they might present some kind of threat.

For the rest of the evening, we tiptoed around it. I did a performative amount of tidying and Joe put a few of the apparently more painful items in one of the boxes he'd brought: a wristwatch with a peeling leather band; a compass in a wooden compact. We ate a quiet dinner of sandwiches while the stream outside chattered in our stead and then an orchestra of night bugs accompanied our retirement to the bedroom. The toilet and sink in the attached bathroom worked, although the water looked a little rusty.

The steel bed springs complained as we slid between the prickly down mattress and the hand-stitched comforter, but were they dutifully accommodating. After the long drive and the longer evening, that antique bed felt like a sepia photograph—dry and dusty, but not without a familiar comfort one could sink into if she had nothing else. I slept like the dead until the ghost came.

How did I know it was a ghost? Well, imagine a windstorm which grows throughout the night. A soft breeze that steadily builds to a gale and, in doing so, invades the sleeper's mind first through dreams, then in restless tossing, until finally, in the bruising funnel of a tornado as the timbers creak and the window frames whine, the dreamer is snatched awake but is already frayed bare from hours of unconscious worry. That was the way in which the ghost announced its presence from the rooftop. It pulled me from unformed nightmares with the hollow stomp of its feet above, moaning, "Junippy paw, Junippy paw. Who, oh, who has got my Junippy paw?"

When I opened my eyes, Joe was already sitting upright, back against the oak headboard and blankets bunched in his fists. The weak light pressing through the curtains rendered the room in submarine blue, and Joe —with his matted hair and wide, white eyes—was a drowned man. My reverie hung for a moment, an odd calm suspended beneath the clatter on the roof and the whine of, "Junippy paw, Junippy paw." Then the front door opened a crack.

The cabin was a shotgun-style so that from the bed we could see straight through the living room to the front door. It began to spread open and Joe tugged the sheets to his chest and the barest whimper escaped him. His breath caught, though, as the door swung fully open to reveal the shaggy outline of the Bernese mountain dog, backlit by the glow from the stars outside.

I couldn't tell at first that anything was wrong with Juniper, other than her being there while—as far I knew—also being dead. As I watched, however, she raised one shaky front paw and swung it forward to cross the threshold. Then a back paw; then the other front; the other back. Creeping step by step, each movement just out of sync with the next, the dog wobbled into the house as if tiptoeing. Despite her size, each movement seemed limp yet ponderous.

As the enormous dog quivered further into the living room, the wind outside shifted and Juniper's fur twitched as the overwhelming smell of wet fur and the cloying sweetness of river mud pressed over us like a second blanket. That same wind must have pushed back the clouds enough for the moon to peer through, too, because just then we saw the long silver threads that sank deep into the dog's flesh. Plucking at her back and buried in each joint and all four paws, gleaming wires disappeared up into the ceiling as if attached to a hidden marionette's cross.

"Junippy paw!"

And the dog leapt straight up as if in a dance. The roof shook with the hop and shuffle like tap shoes above us, and the rancid sack of fur and bones in the living room reeled like a drunkard at the end of those silver lines. With every bounce, the backing choir of wires shrieked and whined.

Joe was out of bed, rushing toward where Juniper hopped, and I was yanked along in his wake by my own fear of being left alone there. Joe crashed headlong into the thicket of wires, but I got only a step beyond the bedroom before the first barb pierced my bare foot. With a shriek, I jumped onto my good foot and pulled the other up to stare at the shiny metal hook in the flesh and at the first drop of blood, black in the dim light, starting to well out. A limp wire, thin as a hair, ran from its eye up into the darkness.

Then Joe screamed and I looked up from my wound. Juniper's carcass had fallen limp, but Joe was also on the floor, rolling beside her in agony.

Wary, I leaned on the doorframe and fished an arm around to paw the living room light switch on. With a flash, all was revealed. Everywhere around us, little silver hooks curled up on every surface or dangled like silk-worms from glistening threads. Their lines ran up toward the ceiling before fading out of sight as if into an impossible distance. I stood there, understanding yet still not comprehending what I saw. So absorbing was the sight that it took a moment to realize the prancing on the roof had stopped. It wasn't silent, but after the cacophony from above, Joe's whimpers were like the drips of rain from the eaves after a storm has moved on. Or, I later realized, when one is in its eye.

In that brief lull, I set to working the hook from my sole. Numbed by adrenaline, it was as if someone else's skin puckered around the metal, and, with dummy hands, I tried to work it out as gingerly as possible. My best wasn't much, though, and I was doing significant damage with the blood now running across the soft skin. Somehow the gash didn't hurt but the flow of blood tickled, and I couldn't help but giggle through the tears.

I had just gotten the arrowhead of the barb free when the wire pulled tight. The tip was still inside and so the hook ripped its way through the rest of me in a long, ragged slice from my midsole to instep. All around, the lines were flying upward like falling stars in reverse and disappearing into nonexistence just at the ceiling's line. The hooting and stomping above us erupted with a renewed and demented glee.

"Junippy paw, Junippy paw," it screamed. "You have got my Junippy paw!"

The roof shook as if punched by a great downward gust, and Joe and Juniper both lifted off the floor, bites of their skin tented upward beneath the sunken teeth of the hooks. The wail that Joe unleashed was in a pitch I'd never heard before. Then Juniper flew out the door on the metal strands and Joe was floating in midair as if waiting to follow.

I admit it. I panicked.

I didn't want him to disappear into the great dark outside. I was at least as scared for myself as for him. So I threw all my weight onto Joe, desperate to ground him and keep him with me.

In my memory, for one brief moment, we are forever suspended in an embrace with mouths open and tears streaming, hanging mid-air like fish breaking from the surface of a stream. Then gravity strikes and the hooks make a sound like feet pulled from sucking mud, and we crash.

Exhaustion must have taken me, because the rest of the night I spent tending our wounds and then waking up alone the next morning don't quite bleed together. In retrospect there is a dividing line, although I struggle to draw it any more clearly than one moment we were together in bed, crying softly, and the next we weren't. I was by myself, twisted up in sheets that bore the blossoms of all our little injuries, and he was gone. The bedroom door was closed.

Rising, I wrapped myself in the God's Eye quilt that covered the raw pine footlocker at the foot of the bed. The wood's rough edges plucked at the yarn as I pulled it away. The musty smell of its age overwhelmed me and set my eyes itching, but it was so cold in the bedroom that I knew the front door was open even before I stepped out into the living room. When I did, frigid morning light was spilling in through the open door. Just beyond the frame, I heard Joe shuffle on the porch, and so I pulled the quilt tighter and headed to him.

Outside, across the yard, the bushes were silver with frozen dew and the stream was smoking as it wound just into and then out of sight. There were still drops of blood on the floor and, as I got to the door, heavy paw prints in black mud that were also rimmed with frost. My breath was smoking like the river, but the morning was clear and, for the first time, I could see the mountains in the distance. Their snow-capped peaks were a knife-sharp profile in recline. Although the morning was bright, a smothering blanket of gray clouds was already crawling up behind us and I knew it would all be gone soon.

Joe was staring off above the tree line and leaning against the rail. I put my arms around him, careful to touch only those spots between the wounds.

"We should leave," I whispered.

I realize now that if ever there was a time when I could have saved him, that was it.

He grunted. "Let's just go back inside."

"We're not safe here," I pressed him.

"I need—" he began, but paused. He cleared his throat. "I need to put this to rest."

"To rest?" I asked.

"Yes. I'm here because this is my—" He stopped. Legacy? Destiny? Fault? But he just shook his head and muttered, "I have to finish it." His voice rose a little when he addressed me again. "Would you really deny me that?"

Had I denied him anything, ever? It would have been simpler, of course, to just leave, but we were so locked into our mutual gravity that what was I going to do? Drive our car, which had been mine, back to our one-bedroom apartment, which had been his? What would I do with that group of acquaintances or grim determinism we both were saddled with and neither enjoyed? What would I do in that strange city where I didn't even have a job, if I didn't have Joe?

All I could do was ask, "How?"

"I'll find whatever it is that's keeping him—I mean, it—here," Joe said. "And then we'll set him free." He turned to look out toward those knife-nosed mountains, now just barely covered by the shroud of fog. "We'll be free."

If I told you I wanted it to be true, would you believe me? If I told you that I hadn't wanted to run, but secretly longed for the kind of crucible that would finally either kill this thing between us dead once and for all, or else forge us into two whole people, even if we shared a common nucleus of horror?

If you don't believe that, what if I told you I was already convincing myself this was just one more thing that wasn't as bad as it looked from the outside?

I nodded. "Okay, let's stay."

We spent the day cleaning, half-heartedly looking for the key to our imprisonment, and not talking about what had happened. Only once did I broach the subject, when Joe had picked up the picture of his grandfather and was frozen there for a full minute, staring down at the hawksbill profile.

"Was it him?" I asked.

Joe looked up at me, then back down to the picture. He shrugged. "It sounded like him, but that's crazy." He looked at me again and I could read it then in his eyes what he was really asking. "Right?"

So I just nodded. "But what was it— What was he saying?"

Joe closed his eyes. "Junippy Paw. That was my name for Juniper when I was a kid."

I didn't want to ask it, but I did. "Why would your dead grandfather use your nickname for his dog?"

Without warning, Joe threw the picture to the floor, and I recoiled as shards of glass sprayed from the broken frame, silver bullets in the light, but I was too startled to speak. Joe went back to the bookshelf and stared at the spines, the conversation over.

But then, to my surprise, he knelt down and picked up the photograph, shaking it clean. He put it into an old shoebox that had materialized from the piles of debris, one marked with a child's size, but which was clearly empty. For the rest of the day, that was Joe's work: moving pictures from frames into the box. Nothing that I could see which would help clear the house or set us free.

———

If you've ever witnessed an explosion and, still shell-shocked, assumed there was no way the fallout could be worse, you'll understand why that second night we bolted the door and wedged a chair beneath the handle. We made earplugs from a tub of beeswax that we found in a kitchen cupboard. In the bedroom, in the darkness, with my heartbeat in my ears, I felt almost insulated enough to ignore the thing stomping on the roof.

Joe and I slept back to back, and when my bladder prodded me awake, I took the flashlight when I got up to use to bathroom and each sweep of the beam revealed little silver hooks crawling over every surface like slugs after a rain. With great care I wove myself around the hair-thin metal lines that disappeared back up into the ceiling. I took a hold of one and plucked it, but if it made a sound before it snapped back up through the ceiling, I couldn't hear it through the wax.

The next morning, I made eggs on the kitchenette range and we ate balanced on the porch railing. Joe picked at his and headed back inside to continue moving relics from one corner of the cabin to another and back again, ostensibly looking for a key to our interminable haunting. I lingered outside, contemplating how the mountains that I had seen so clearly the day before now only suggested themselves behind the gray curtain of the horizon.

Shortly after coming back in, I was taking down the stuffed owl from the bookshelf when I found the old box of shells for the shotgun by the closet. The box rattled when I shook it, the heavy red plastic cases tumbling over one another like beetles. One by one, I stood the shells up on the shelf at eye level: four stout hunters that Joe couldn't help but see as he moved around the room. He never mentioned them, though, so they sat there like more little scabs we wouldn't discuss.

Let me tell you that I could have dealt with anger. I could have dealt with sadness, even fear. I wanted it! But instead, Joe flitted through his dead grandfather's house like a ghost himself, content to plug his ears and let us pick our way around silver fishhooks every night. It felt untenable.

Throughout our time together, I had been forced to be the decisive one, whether it was fair or not. So, that third night, as the sun began to sink, I bundled myself as heavily as I could and limped out on my bad foot into the trees just beyond the house's clearing. If Joe missed me, it wasn't enough to get him out looking. My only company, the shotgun, lay beside me on the God's Eye quilt I'd spread over the ground, its barrel glistening under a new sheen of oil. The vivid pink and orange of the sunset's reflection had skimmed along the metal surface like an artist's rendering of gunpowder combustion, although the glow burned off into darkness soon enough.

The moon rose, but still I waited. Almost cozy in all my protective layers, I even dozed a bit as I sat against the far side of a cedar trunk, but I rose quickly when I heard the clopping on the cabin roof. I lifted the shotgun's stock to my shoulder and leaned out from around the tree.

The ghost was hopping from foot to foot across the roof like a great barn owl and hooting: "Junippy Paw! Junippy Paw! Who, oh, who's got my Junippy Paw!" Then he looked right at me, his horrible face like a knife in the new moonlight. Its kinship with the faded pictures Joe had shown me was uncanny. I rested the shotgun's sight just below its chest, where its heart should be, and inhaled.

I exhaled slowly and pulled the trigger.

The night shook and the flash from the barrel blew out my aiming eye for a moment. I heard the grunt of the shot hit and, with my good eye, I watched the thing's arms fly out wide like wings about to lift off, but instead he careened over the far side of the roof's peak. Even above the ringing in my ears, I heard the meaty slap when it hit the ground on the opposite side.

I popped the shotgun's breech and let the burnt shells fly. I fixed the last two good ones in place and headed around the cabin, fully expecting to find just empty ground. A blood trail, perhaps, to lure me off into the woods like poisoned breadcrumbs. What I wasn't expecting, though, was the body that was still there.

His cheeks were covered with a layer of downy feathers. In the distance it had looked like a mask, but now up close and with the beak clearly visible, it was somewhere halfway between a grandfather and a bird. I prodded one of its arm-wings with the shotgun barrel, spreading it out. It ended in four long-nailed fingers with coils of silver thread spooled around each digit and passels of little silver hooks tucked beneath. Its glossy eyes were half open, but the lifeless stare wasn't the jet black of a raven or the yellow of an owl. Instead, they had a hazel ring around the pupil. Little rosebuds of blood welled up from the holes across the blue-black skin of its torso.

"Honey?" Joe called from inside. Even through the closed window I sensed his panic and it stirred me. "What's happening?"

"I got him," I called out, then corrected myself. "It. I got it."

I was still trying to take in all the body's strange details when Joe came outside. He gasped when he saw it and turned away quickly, wrapping his arms across his chest as if bound. I stepped to him and fumbled into a one-armed hug even as I still held the shotgun in the other hand, ready to point it. The grip was cumbersome, but I didn't dare put the gun down.

"You killed him," Joe whispered into my shoulder.

"It," I mumbled.

We covered the body with the God's Eye quilt, but the little blooms of blood still seeped through. Joe couldn't bring himself to touch the corpse, but when I finally picked it up, it was lighter than I'd expected. It felt as if its bones were hollow, easy enough to carry, but since I was burdened, Joe took our Coleman lantern in one hand and the shotgun in the other and led us out into the woods. With each swing, the light made cage bars from the shadows of the trunks and branches, then let the flat darkness erase them. He stopped when we finally reached a small dip in the ground beside the elbow of the stream.

With a grunt, I lay the bundle down on damp leaves just beyond the crook. I looked around for rocks or branches or something to cover it, but there was nothing suitable.

"Here's good enough?" I asked.

Joe turned and looked back toward the cabin, but it was too obscured to give any light. He shrugged. As if in answer, something large broke the water's surface behind us and splashed back into the depth.

"Should we say something, maybe?" I asked.

In the lantern's glow, Joe's face was fixed like a mask. If he shot me right then, would he even blink, I wondered.

"Like what?" he asked.

"Never mind," I said. One end of the quilt had slid up as I walked and revealed the creature's five long toes. On their own, exposed, the thick yellow nails looked brittle, and I couldn't wait to leave it there on the ground behind us. "Let's just go."

———

We slept that night without earplugs. I lay on my side to face Joe with one arm draped across his chest like a seatbelt. Even then I knew I couldn't hold on to him forever, but I couldn't yet give up trying. Still, the world outside invaded my dreams. The trees groaned in the wind and night bugs bickered and hummed in conspiracy. Although the cabin had no wind chime, a metallic hum always felt as if it rested just on the edge of my hearing. I was frayed and worried even as I slept.

I woke shivering. My feet were numb and heavy like boots filled with water. Without opening my eyes, I pressed against Joe, trying to intertwine our legs so that I could feel the prickle of his hairs against my skin, but he was cold, too, and still. My hand on his chest, I felt half-breaths slipping in and out like a ghost failing to rise from a shallow grave. Inevitably, I opened my eyes.

When I did, the bedroom door was open and across the cabin the front door was open and, beyond that, the mist rising from the ground obscured anything that lay outside the frame. As my eyes adjusted, however, I could see the clotted tracks of mud which paced from the porch outside right up to foot of the bed. They ended right beside Joe and, just for a moment, I was taken with the notion that some great man-shaped emptiness watched us as we lay there. But that was crazy, right?

Unable to contain my revulsion, I flung the bedspread from our feet with a great burst like a limp wing flapping once before collapsing to the floor. In that moment, of course, I thought I would expose muddy soles and grass between toes. Perhaps a silver hook still in a heel. I would finally be able to point the finger.

But no.

The bedclothes between us were equally ruined. In the dim light, the white sheets were again submarine blue, the mud was black, and yet I couldn't disentangle what I saw. The muck had been so spread and smeared by our restless thrashing and unconscious entanglement that we were both indistinguishably soiled. A rat's nest bale of silver wire lay just beyond our toes with its myriad hooks gripping the linen like toenails, surprised at being discovered and desperate not to be removed. One mottled pinion feather protruded from its coils almost as if it was hatching.

I hesitated at the thought of waking Joe. What would he even say?

For a moment I lay there, looking at our dirty feet wrapped in the sheets. Would he admit that it was him? Would he tell me that he had lost control? Would he blame the thing that had always been between us, but which this trip had finally raised up?

Or would he blame the thing we left lying on the ground out beyond the crook of the stream?

Or would he say that it had been me? At that point, alone and in the dark, I couldn't be sure it wasn't.

I rose, unsure of where I would go or what I would do, but unable to share the bed any longer. The bundle of wire and feather still lying there at the foot again caught my eye as it gleamed. It was the size of both of my fists, maybe, and I was again taken with the fancy that it looked like an egg. The wires of its surface glistened and shadows seemed to flow down the single protruding feather like ink spilling backward out of a quill, swirling just beneath its surface.

It was a madness, I sometimes tell myself. An undiagnosable melancholy, perhaps. But I couldn't bear to leave it. Instead, I went back to the living room and found Joe's shoebox full of old photos. I emptied it out and left the pictures next to the now-empty box of shotgun shells, the last live rounds still in the gun itself, which slept again by the closet door.

Back in the bedroom, I tenderly lifted the wire egg and found it was lighter than I'd expected. I turned it in my hands, avoiding the hooks while I tried to follow the silver thread as it looped and curled around on itself. Just beneath the deepest layer of coils, I thought I saw something shiny at the center of it and, against my better judgment, I pressed my thumbs down into the folds and pulled, trying to spread it just enough to see.

Numbed from the chill, my fingers slipped, and one of the hooks dug into my thumb. With a yelp I let go but it clung for just a moment, latched into me, then it released and fell into the box with a thud and a gentle tinkle like a chime. Joe groaned in his sleep, and as I sucked on my injured thumb, I tasted something sour beneath the rich copper of my blood.

Joe stirred again but didn't wake, clenching and dropping the sheet, each grasp leaving little tracks across the fabric. Moving to his side, I lifted his closest hand. It felt so heavy, twice the size of mine almost, but the palm was puckered with the little mouths of wounds. I began to kneel, willing the cuts to be leftover scars and not the fresh, bleeding injuries actually before me, but as I did, the fecal, rotting smell of the mud grew stronger. Finally, when my face was only inches from his palm and I saw the long dark hairs punched into the angry holes, I could also finally discern another smell beneath the muck. I reached beneath the bed, into the pool of shadow like a catfish noodler, and my fingertips confirmed the source—wet dog.

I realized that if ever there was a time that I had to save myself, that was it.

I rose without looking. The knees of my pajamas dampened by the dark water pooling out from under the bed, I gathered my things. Even as I threw what I could into my bag and took my car keys from his jeans, I couldn't penetrate Joe's slumber. I considered waking him—I honestly did—but the black, brown, and white bulk beneath the bed kept me away. So, I left.

As I stepped out of the bedroom, the refinished wall called to me. The dull spots of filler were like bad stars against the lacquer of the undamaged wood, but there, next to the half-size door into the thicket of rods and brooms, sat the shotgun. Two fresh shells, the last in the house, waited in its throat like the final words in an argument. I wasn't going to do it, no; but the barrels leaned there like church organ pipes, still resonating in a requiem that I couldn't quite hear.

So, I cracked the breech. Of all the things I would leave Joe with—easy or hard—this wasn't it. I took all the shells in the house with me.

All the ones I knew of, I mean. Honest.

Outside, a raccoon sat on the far porch railing, rubbing its hands together as if plotting. Its amber eyes sparkled behind the inky domino mask above its sharp muzzle. Then it crawled down to the lawn and disappeared into the shadows. I slammed the cabin door behind me and stepped off into the gravel.

———

Gordon B. White

So, yes. I left Joe there. I left him to wake, perhaps, and wait for his true wife to emerge from the woods, her face as sharp as a beak and fingers strong as birch. Or maybe to sit with his Junippy Paw beside him on the porch until he finally grew his own feathers and flew away. Or maybe just until he followed his black dog down to the bend of the river and let it hold them both beneath the crook of its arm.

Whatever was coming for him, I drove off into the morning alone and waited until I crossed the state line to throw those last two shotguns shells out the window and off onto the shoulder. I took my car back to his apartment and then I packed my clothes and personal effects, after which I left his mother's ring on the counter next to the keys to his front door and went back to my family. And now, yes, years later, I'm over it.

Sometimes, though, when my husband now is away and my children are gone, I take the old shoebox from under the bed. It smells faintly of damp cardboard and something sweeter, and it's always lighter than I expect. I shake it, just a little, to hear the tinkle of silver wire and the vane and barbs of a thick pinion feather brush back and forth inside like the hint of a wing. Then, with a sigh, I put it away for now.

Hearth and Home

As I steered her toward the grumbling hearth, the purple silk veiling the hole of her face trembled. She hooted like a nightbird: "So cold, my son. So cold."

The thing that kept claiming to have been our mother sank onto dirt-caked knees and lamb-white hands, then dutifully crawled inside.

"You must come too," she wailed. "To check the windows and latch the doors."

I nudged the trim of her funeral clothes inside and closed the grate. An orange tongue licked the damp hem, hissed, then tiny red teeth bit in.

"This is your little house now, Mother. Stay warm."

Devil Take Me

The caveat is that I'm going to lie to you. That's how confessions work, isn't it? There are those things that even though we want to confess, we can't confront, and so we talk around. Lying isn't even second nature; it's our primary condition. The best I can do is tell you the truth about when I've lied.

Let's start at the beginning. I come from a deep and worn-out notch on the Bible Belt, the only child of Peter and Trudy Cadigan. Well, no. You'd need only look at the graves to know that's not entirely true. While I can't promise I'll fix every misstatement, allow me to clarify that I am their first-born son and their only surviving child. Adam was the other.

Please forgive the confusion, but there are certain moments in life, it seems, that blind you to the others. Perhaps the rest of life is duller than these bright peaks of experience, and so only they stand out. I worry that maybe those spikes of experience are so deeply affecting that they gouge the eyes of memory and wiggle around like icepicks until nothing is left in the brain but the singular moments. It makes me wonder what I've lost, both good and bad.

Whatever else you take from me, though, this part is absolutely true: There was something wicked in our house. A darkness grew like mold from the baseboards and hung like lichen from the walls. It stitched itself together in empty closets and the shadows behind bedroom doors until, one night, it took solid form.

————

Although I was very young, I remember the day Mama told me my little brother Adam was growing in her belly. I remember because my father loved to tease me about how I cried for a solid week. He found it funny, but I choose to believe that even then, I was already sorry for the thing that was growing in the middle of our family.

Would you believe I was not a typical child? I didn't, for example, have much of a dinosaur phase. I didn't watch cartoons. Instead, by the time Adam was growing inside Mama, I had become obsessed with wounds. Scraped knees; the jelly jar incident; Sundays staring at Christ on the cross. A hundred little injuries harrowed into me a preoccupation with holes in flesh: skin and muscle curling like lips; a public intimacy; a Möbius strip. The interior and exterior as one.

Even at that age, I was possessed of the mystical thought that a wound was the structure of infinity. If I moved forward in time—a year, a dozen, a hundred—I would find the same wound on the same body, still ringing in time. If I could move backward, I wondered, would I find it there, too, just waiting to be uncovered?

Years later, I read about a famous author who said his stories were like dinosaur skeletons: pre-existent but buried, merely waiting on the chisel and brush. Stories are not created by writing, in other words, but excavated in the telling. Stories are always underfoot whether we believe in them or not. Whatever names we give, whatever order we impose, it's all just guesses.

But if that were true, then who could we blame for the stories we find ourselves written into? Who bears the burden when bad things happen that we don't deserve?

Who wrote the dinosaurs, is what I'm asking, and why must we live in prisons of dead monsters' bones?

———

If I say Daddy was a brute, certain images arise. Rolled sleeves; dirty nails; hands perpetually curling toward a fist or a bottle's neck. Glassy eyes; leaden brow. I could tell you that was true, and that things always simply look like what they are, and that would be a comfortable lie. But no, my father was boring like a package bomb.

As proof, I offer you one of those memorial peaks that flatten the rest. We were sitting on the brown couch, Daddy and I, which means we were watching football or the news. Whatever Daddy was watching, I was picking at one threadbare armrest, absorbed in unravelling its awful pattern. It didn't matter what we watched; being near him was almost like being a part of something. I remember Daddy was drinking Coca-Cola from a jelly jar.

Maybe you recall how companies used to decorate jelly jars with popular cartoon characters so that mothers would wash them out and keep them as drinking glasses for children. That's how ingrained associations work, right? Sustenance and entertainment; thanking the jelly company during Grace at every meal; watching the goggle-eyed decal thinning away from wash after wash until only the ghost of its outline remains.

Of all our makeshift vessels, the one in Daddy's hand bore a purple brontosaurus. As he raised the glass, the dinosaur's long neck extended from beneath Daddy's fingers to leer at me with big white eyes and a toothless smile, nodding up and down as my father drank. In between sips, it perched with pride on the couch's arm.

Mama had entered the living room as part of her *tidying up*, although Mama's *tidying* was worrying set in motion. She had mastered a humming-bird's dip and dart, weaving her swelling belly around and beneath Daddy's attention as she pecked and fussed at clutter. She moved through his space almost unseen, although the dinosaur on Daddy's jelly glass leered at her with open-mouthed awe, until the gravity of growing Adam must have depressed the joists beneath the living room's hardwood floor just enough to tip the television antenna's precarious balance.

The image on the screen crumbled, hissing as it thrashed itself into static.

"Christ, Trudy," Daddy hollered. "Can't you do that somewhere else?"

Mama scuttled to the rabbit ears atop the set, trying to wrestle the picture back onto the screen. "It's a mess out here," she muttered, still fiddling.

"The boy and I are trying to relax and watch TV," Daddy said. "You're ruining it."

"Is that right?" she asked me, but I turned my attention back to the armrest. I had learned the hard way not to let them argue through me.

Daddy began grumbling in a prelude to further shouting, and Mama froze, but in that moment the alignment was restored. The image was clear and the sound returned. I recall now that the local news was on, and next to the anchor flashed a picture of a house on fire. *Tragedy*, read the caption.

Daddy fell silent and Mama gently let go and the picture stayed. She took a careful step back, then shook her head—not at us, but at everything—and, for a moment, just stood there. Then she sighed and said, "I'll leave you to it."

As she left the living room, passing my end of the couch on her way out and down the hall, she bent down and gave me a quick peck on the cheek. It was barely a graze, and then she was gone.

Do I really remember that soft and fleeting touch? Or is it just a counterpoint I fabricated to balance what came next?

Craning my neck around to watch Mama disappear down the hallway and into my parents' bedroom, something bit me.

I squealed and flailed at the sudden pain, but my hands found only Daddy's heavy, hairy hand. Startled, I turned as much as I could. With a fold of skin from just below my ribs pinched between his knuckle and thumb, he grinned as he twisted and wrung another howl from me.

"Don't be so soft." He squeezed harder.

Sobbing now, I batted at Daddy's hand, but his grip was unrelenting. Down the hall, in that distant doorway, a shape that must have been Mama hovered just on the edge. Unable—or unwilling—to leave that safety, it beckoned to me.

I mule-kicked backward against Daddy's grip. My heel sank into the soft gut just over-lipping his belt and, with a noise between a heave and a gasp, all the breath left him. His pinch suddenly released, but a wave of gravity washed over us, and time froze, and I felt the port of air around us on the verge of collapse.

A crash. The jelly jar shattering. The cartoon dinosaur blasting into a hundred pieces, each one dancing across the wooden floor and into the shadows beneath the couch.

"Oh, god—" But Daddy bit down the curse like a bug, his lips curling with the bitterness. He reached over to snatch at me, but I was already standing as if to run.

"Well?" He pointed those long, evil fingers at where the jelly jar had crashed like a meteor from the couch's arm A few larger pieces of the wreckage were plain, but most were just glints in the dim light and the dark, sticky spray of Coca-Cola. By reflex, I opened my mouth to call for Mama, but Daddy sneered me silent.

"Don't drag your mother into this," he hissed. "A man takes responsibility for his actions. You clean it up."

When I tell you I did it—that I cleaned it all up—do you picture me, age five, getting the broom and dustpan from the hall closet? Do you imagine me finding a paper bag for the bigger glass pieces, then heading down into the cellar to pull an old t-shirt from the rag shelf in order to wipe up the soda and those splinters of glass almost too small to see? Was I mature beyond my years?

Or do you see me, bruised by the weight of all my father's attention, my mother a shadow in a doorway, as I kneel and scrape? Am I too afraid to leave for even a second, so that I pick up jelly jar shards and hold them in a cupped hand as the edges cut my fingers and palm, and the tiniest bits work their way beneath my skin? Are my hands bleeding and does the severed head of the purple cartoon dinosaur grin up at me from the broken pieces?

I won't tell you which way it was, but believe me when I tell you that even if I couldn't see it, the wicked thing was in the house that day. That it hid down a dark hallway; that it stalked behind a screen of television static; that it coiled beneath the couch, lapping at spilled Coca-Cola.

And what if I told you, too, that it was around this time that the darkness in the house became more concrete? That at night, as my father's snores rattled the house's thin walls, the shadows in the hallway pulsed in time. That as I hid beneath my blankets, picking scabs, I heard the floorboards creak, the peel and pop of sticky footsteps circling around. That I felt the weight of the absence of light lower itself onto the foot of my bed.

Wouldn't that be something?

———

If I say my mother was a sad woman, it conjures a particular picture. You probably envision her with long, matted hair, as if she hadn't risen from bed for a week. Or perhaps she sits forever beside a window, wrists and ankles crossed, tears brimming like raindrops on the eaves. And these might not be inaccurate, but I also remember her in the sun, arms bare, hair cut short, laughing and smiling. In hindsight, though, I wonder if that memory is too bright?

For example, I have a flash of her at a Sunday social on the lawn behind our church's Family and Life Center. It could have been right around when Adam started growing, but I don't think I'd yet been told. The afternoon was brilliant and humid; the grass so high you could smell it beneath the vinegar tang of the barbecue. I was sitting at a picnic table next to Daddy, picking at a hole in the plasticized shell of the checkered tablecloth, teasing out strands of its inner fluff, when my father grabbed my hand.

"Quit scratching at things all the dang time," he said. "Why're you always ruining other people's stuff?"

"Sorry," I muttered, and he released me.

"Go find your mother," he said. "I'm done."

Mama's seat across from us was empty. A blue Solo cup rimmed by kiss marks and a chewed-over thigh bone on a styrofoam plate were the only evidence she had been there. The only evidence other than us, I mean.

I left Daddy to weave through the crowd of adults and the few other children. I felt no animosity, really, but I knew that people were generally happier if I wasn't there for them to have to ignore.

I found Mama drifting away from the crowd, arms stretched out, there in the expanse of grass between the picnic area's concrete slab and the woods beyond. She was craning her neck like a featherless bird and had lost her shoes somewhere. Her sundress was the same yellow as the buttercups and wild dandelions burning in the midday sun, and it looked as much like she was summoning those bright weeds around her as it did like she was falling to pieces.

"Mama?" I called out. A dense humidity clotted the air, though, and each golden-petalled head between us seemed a landmine, so I hung back. When she didn't respond, I shouted: "Mama!"

Now, a child shouting "Mama" should turn every mother's head. It should pull them up from cornbread and sweet tea. It should reel them out of bed and down dark hallways. It should bring them back from the fields where brilliant dandelions burn before turning ash-white and blowing away, instead of ignoring their sons until, gripped in frenzy, those sons wail for them from the picnic tables.

I would like to tell you that my mother returned to me immediately. That wrapped in her bare arms, I could smell the sun on her skin. That she was always smiling.

But that fabric falls apart when I pick at the strands, because I remember her, too, with long sleeves over yellowing dime-sized bruises. Forever *tidying*, bobbing up and down just beneath the surface of Daddy's attention. In the church's pew, arms crossed over her swelling belly in a succession of Sundays. Then worn down, thinner and thinner, after Adam came.

"We have our lot in life," Mama would say. *Our lot.* In my mind, those words have become entwined with the Bible story of Lot and his wife, who turned into a pillar of salt. You might recall that Lot and his family fled from the filth of Sodom and Gomorrah just as the Lord put the match to it, and how the angels had warned, *"Don't you look back."* But Lot's wife did look back and for that she was punished. The moral is: if you don't listen to God, if you can't help but look back, or have second thoughts or questions? *Boom.* Salt.

But maybe you'll remember, too, that earlier, Lot's house had been beset by a rapacious mob demanding Lot turn out his guests—angels in disguise—so they could be ravished. Instead, Lot offered the crowd his virgin daughters. Well, the mob declined, but the angels said to Lot, *"Thanks for trying, old man. Now, God is going to do some smiting, but your reward is a slight head start before He ends your fucking world with fire."*

Can you imagine doing all of that—living virtuously amid sin, sheltering angels, and even offering your innocents to the heathens—only to be told that everything is going to burn anyway? And that your reward is to strike out into the desert to start again, forever fearing that someday another angel might come to torch it all once more?

And so sometimes I wonder if maybe, as they fled, Lot's poor, nameless wife had some misgivings, rousted as she was out of her house by angels and dragged along by the man who'd just that night tried to throw her daughters to the jackals. It makes me wonder if, when Lot's wife turned back around, it wasn't a hesitance to leave wickedness behind, but a firm rejection of that future with Lot and his God stretching out before her.

I wonder, too, if she tasted the salt of her own tongue as she turned. If she felt like she was falling into ten million tiny pieces, or if she finally felt whole and pure as crystal? Punishments are only punishments when you want something different, I suppose. Same for rewards, I'd wager, and acts of mercy, too.

———

It might sound like a lie, but I don't remember much of Adam beyond the shadow he cast from between the bars of his crib in Mama and Daddy's room. It isn't fair, but I think of him in terms of absences and what he took away.

Daddy brought Gramma Joy-Anne to stay with me when he took Mama to the hospital. For two days, the house had baking bread and frying chicken, songs during the day and stories at night. It's not that Mama and Daddy never did those things, but rather that those particular moments have become emblematic of my life before Adam. I have trouble not feeling like he took this from me.

And Mama? She was always cold after the baby was born. Beginning while she was pregnant, Mama grew her hair long to cover the back of her neck and hang over her eyes. She wore long sleeves in the summer, and I recall her as always under a blanket. Even though it never really got *cold* where we lived, Mama dug an old kerosene space heater out of the cellar and every night she ran it in the room she and Daddy and Adam all shared. From my room, I heard its wheeze and saw the orange glow seeping from beneath their door into the dark hallway.

As for Daddy, whatever spark he'd had—kind or cruel—went out. For days at a stretch, he wouldn't talk to us at all, not even to say, "Good morning" or "Leave me alone." His eyes were glassy, and once, as he and I sat on the brown couch eating TV dinners and he was drinking Coca-Cola from a mason jar, I watched the last of it go. There was a brief smoldering and then a flare as some enormous emotion contorted his brow from beneath his skin and I cringed into the corner, sure he was going to explode, but no. His face merely collapsed, slack and dark.

We were all exhausted because, more than anything, what the baby stole was any sense of peace. All evening, hour after hour, he yowled like a cat that saw a ghost. He'd tire himself out around when I was put to bed, but sure as stars, he'd start up again around midnight, tearing through the house's walls like a bull's horn.

I'd like to say I am ashamed that at night I'd pray to God to grant peace to the screaming baby, but after I said "*Amen,*" I'd twist my hands upside down. At that age, I thought my clasped hands were an antenna, and so with the steeple of my fingers inverted, I'd whisper beneath the baby's wails,

"Dear Devil, please take him away." Somewhere in Hell, I imagined a television set flickering to life to show me sinning on its screen.

Now, some folks say the Devil is real and walks among us. Others say it was made up by men as an excuse—or at least a reason—as to why they do bad things. If that was the case, though, what would you make the Devil out of? The pieces you have handy, I'd wager.

———

I can offer you one final night at a party in a garden, the last evening of the fall. Another potluck church social, congregants arrayed at the picnic tables behind the Family and Life Center. Reverend Mott pressed and flipped hamburgers on the grill, while bowls of green beans, macaroni, and four types of potatoes sat nearby to distract the flies. Sweating gallon jugs of sweet tea lounged next to plastic cups, although the bags of ice had long since melted. The smell of sizzling meat and the buzz of conversation filled the air.

My family, however, sat in weary quiet at a table on the gathering's outer ring: Mama, Daddy, Adam in his carrier, and me. Evening had settled down around us, and although strings of holiday lights crisscrossed overhead, our table was just far enough from the center that everything was dim. I had eaten and was sitting quietly, staring out into the distance, and Adam was mercifully sleeping. Mama and Daddy mostly just looked past each other across the table, every now and then speaking softly. Their voices buzzed like the gentle waves of a television tuned almost too low to hear, and I was beginning to drift.

Daddy took a sip from a red plastic Solo cup and set it down. From the corner of my eye, I saw Mama reach for it, but just as her fingertips touched it, Daddy placed his hand over the top.

"Give me a sip," Mama said, smiling as if it was a joke.

Daddy shook his head. "Go get your own."

"Why?"

"Cause it's mine."

Mama's smile didn't leave, but it tightened. "You promised you wouldn't."

He stared at her. "I'm not."

"Then give me a sip." She grabbed at the cup, but like a snake striking, Daddy's other hand pinned her wrist to the table.

"I said, don't drink that."

"Why not?" With a grunt, Mama pushed against him, but Daddy held her there.

There was a long moment before he answered. "You know why. You're—"

"I won't be." She let go and twisted her slim wrist out from under from his palm. She stood up and was loud. "Not again or anymore. I can't keep on like this."

Daddy pushed himself up from the picnic table too. "Keep it together in front—"

"In front of him?" She pointed at me and laughed, but it was too bright. "Or him?" Now pointing at Adam. "Or, or—"

"The neighbors," Daddy hissed. I looked around and he was right; the lot of them were already doing a mighty poor job of pretending not to stare.

Mama flashed all her teeth. "Let them watch."

But Daddy moved quickly around the table to take Mama by the arm and half push, half drag her out beyond the lights, leaving Adam and me alone. They stumbled out into that brittle, balding field where once bright yellow buttercups and dandelions had grown. Too far away to hear, in the dying light my parents might almost have been dancing, arms on one another, small steps swaying them out into the darkness. The trees beyond them swayed, too, as if some great beast was moving through the forest just out of sight.

Would you believe, too, that they had just left it there on the table—the red Solo cup that started this all? Well, my curiosity got the better of me. I picked it up, only to be disappointed when I found it was just Coca-Cola. But no, that wasn't quite right, because as I tipped my nose closer, a whiff of something like woodsmoke beneath the surface gave me pause.

I took a sip and nearly gagged. The soda had gone flat and syrupy, but it burned in my throat. Later, I grew to know spirits, but right then all I knew was that beneath the cloying sweetness, I tasted smoldering oak, and it kindled a heat that filled my chest.

As it worked its way through me, the holiday bulbs above burned brighter, swelling up like full moons. The patio grill glowed like Mama's kerosene heater and the world started to lose its hard edges. I took another deep pull from the Solo cup and this time welcomed the fire. Everything around became so bright the shadows all receded up into the sky. Even Adam's face began to beam like a beacon, so bright that it seemed perhaps I might finally, truly see my brother.

I raised the cup once more, only this time it exploded in my grip. I stared at my wounded hand in shock, then looked up to see my father next to me, his hand already raised for a second smack. It took a split second for the sting itself to hit me, and then I squealed.

"You little shit." He grabbed me by the injured hand and squeezed. All the old scars, little white ridges left from the jelly jar shards and its cartoon dinosaur, were seized with a new pain as he crushed them into a single ball of agony.

"Stop that!" Now Mama was pushing Daddy, her voice high and on the verge of breaking. "This is your fault!"

Daddy flinched, but then shoved me aside to grab Mama by the arms again.

"I told you, not in front of—"

But then Adam wailed behind us, and I remember that Daddy spun around and howled too, screaming right back in the baby's face. Of all the commotion, that final outburst was so shocking that everyone and everything went silent, even the night bugs and Adam himself. We all just hung there.

Then the world cracked right open.

It was Adam screaming, people moving and talking, other babies hollering, and me being pulled to and fro by who knows whose hands. In all the bright chaos, the warmth in my stomach went sour. The vapors burned, and I recall the overwhelming sensation that everything inside was coming out.

And then it did: Coca-Cola; hamburgers; potato salad; darkness. Everything. All of it bubbled up inside me and I surrendered, retching, sinking into the shadows.

———

After that are only bits and pieces as my little head bobbed in the dark lake of *Drunk*. Me over Daddy's shoulder, looking back at the sad choir of neighbors, their lips frozen in a hymn of gossip. My head in Mama's lap in the backseat, sprawled out from my wounded hands and belly. My face in the bathroom mirror as Mama scrubbed my chin and Daddy behind us, filling the doorway. And then me in bed, in pajamas, with Mama and Daddy standing just outside the doorway, the light so dim that their faces looked like holes.

Then Adam screaming from the other room, pulling them away. And me, trying to hold onto that one thread of connection before slipping back into the darkness.

———

I woke up in bed, my mouth still syrupy and my throat burned raw. The house was as near as it came to quiet, Adam having screamed himself to temporary sleep and the darkened walls gently vibrating with the kerosene heater's hum and Daddy's snore. I don't know whether some disturbance in the air or in my gut woke me, but I was looking out into the hallway when the orange glow oozing from beneath Mama and Daddy's door quivered. Then I heard them: soft, wet footsteps coming down the hall, each one a little like it was sucking through mud. Pulling the covers to my chin and half-closing my eyes, I pretended to sleep, willing whatever was out there to pass me by.

The footsteps stopped outside my door.

Near the top of the frame, a tiny face peeked around the corner, and then its long, thin neck followed. The little round head and preposterous neck swayed into my room like a snake standing upright, skirting the ceiling and dripping with cobwebs of shadow. Its yellow eyes flashed bright, and the outline of its mouth split into a toothless grin.

At first, I thought it was an enormous serpent, but then a tiny hand with long fingers gripped the side of the doorframe. As it leaned around the edge, the neck connected into rounded shoulders and its squat, naked body slowly emerged. Teetering on stubby legs, arms out to the side for balance, the monster walked into my room.

"Hello," it whispered. "I got your messages."

Pretense abandoned, I threw the covers over my head and curled up like a fetus. Trembling, I tried to remember every prayer, any prayer, but all the words fled my stupid tongue. Step by step, I heard the monster cross the floor and then it sat down on the bed beside me. The mattress springs sighed beneath its weight, and I slid down to rest against the heat of its body. I began to sweat, and when I finally had to let go of the breath I was holding, the thing's odor overwhelmed me. It didn't smell like sulfur, as I'd have imagined, but instead like spilled Coca-Cola left out in the sun, evaporated down to syrup and buzzing with yellowjackets. Beneath that odor, though, was the hint of greasy fat burning on a charcoal grill.

"I'm the Devil," it said as it shifted on the bed, settling in. "Why don't you pop your head out and see?" Its soft voice came from up toward the ceiling, and the edges of its words faded across the distance like the garble of television static. The peripheral hiss pulled a wire in my skin and my hairs stood up like antennae.

When I didn't answer, the Devil sighed. The covers shifted beneath the Devil's hand, and I watched from beneath as the spindly fingers outside pinched the fabric. The Devil gave a gentle tug, but I have never held onto anything as tightly as those blankets. The Devil gave a little chuckle and let go.

"That's fair, I suppose," it said. "We don't need to look at each other to see eye to eye." The Devil moved again, reclining until its pudgy body was lying beside me on the mattress. I felt its long neck coil around, up over my head and then down my back. When the Devil spoke next, the voice came from down at my feet.

"What if I could take away the shadow? If I could leave you with so much light, you almost couldn't bear to look right at it?" the Devil asked. "All you have to do is tell me you want me to do it."

I didn't answer.

The Devil sighed again, its hot breath now between my toes. "Just give me your darkness."

It draped one arm around me from the front while its long neck encircled me. I curled tighter, trying to make myself into a stone, but I could feel its tiny head nuzzling in face first beneath me, worming its way under the blankets. I thrashed against it, but the Devil's arm held me like a seat belt and its neck coiled tighter.

"Give it to me," the Devil grunted, mouth muffled by the sheets as it pushed up by my ankles. It hissed, and a raspy tongue licked across my heel. "Tell me I can have it!"

With that contact, my self-control shattered, and I screamed, and the Devil immediately vanished. Like a bubble popped, all of it was gone: the heat, the weight, the syrupy smell. It left me there, alone, perspiring, the echo of my shout still ringing in my ears.

And yet, when I try now to recall exactly what I had yelled while under the weight of the Devil, I know I had meant to scream "Go away!" although I can't say for sure I got it all out. I didn't have a chance to reflect on it at the time, however, because a second later Adam started howling in the other room.

A second after that, I smelled the brimstone.

———

They say the old kerosene heater must have tipped. Just *boom*, right up in a ball of flame. It had been plugged in by Mama and Daddy's bedroom door and, well, that was that. The door was closed, and so there was no way out into the hall for my family, but not for the flames either. Lucky me.

They found Daddy by the bedroom window, which the firemen reckoned was him looking for a way out. What else could he be doing but trying to help Mama and Adam escape? Mama herself was draped over the crib, holding onto what was left of Adam, and it brought a tear to every eye to think of her reaching for her baby as the flames licked her heels. What else could she have been doing, but trying to snatch him away?

As for me, I had smelled the smoke and heard the screams. Without looking back, I ran outside, barefoot through the grass to the O'Neil family next door. I watched with them from their porch as the fire engines rolled in, wailing like babies, and my house went up in flames, my family with it.

And that was that.

I never saw them again except in my dreams. There, they are whole again, but made of ashes white as salt, frozen in the moments I remember: Daddy on the couch; Mama in a field of dandelions; Adam in his crib. So perfectly are they held there, that I don't dare to breathe for fear of knocking them over.

But then the wind blows, and the ashes scatter like smoke, and when the smoke clears, I am back standing on the O'Neils' porch. My feet are damp from the dew and the coldness is setting in from my toe tips and the bottom of my soles. The fire trucks are still down the block, crying out, but then the house of my childhood erupts into a pillar of fire so bright that the tall, skinny trees behind it are lit up like daylight and finally, in the terrible illumination, I can almost see the thing that did this.

That's the truth, and the Devil take me if I'm lying.

In the Pines

The family is gathered at the mountain house, seated around the dinner table and about to toast Tessa with her favorite Montepulciano, when she gasps from her seat at the head. Her husband, Callum, and her brother, David, leap from their chairs on either side with hands out like spotters. David's wife, Shara, watches the commotion and steals a nervous sip of the full-bodied red before placing her glass down. Relegated to the far end like children, youngest sister, Kels, and her current boyfriend, Burke, quietly exchange a glance, but then turn to look as Tessa points past them, through the sliding glass door, to the naked man creeping on all fours across the lawn.

On most nights, the dining room's view is a Western sweep that would make a pioneer blush. It opens onto a porch settled by Adirondack rockers and potted ornamentals, then a few short steps descend to the lawn Tessa and Callum had clear-cut from the surrounding pines. The sod rolls out to a steep decline, beyond which the purpling sky and shadowed valley spread toward a far, dark knuckle of mountains. For an hour this afternoon, Callum had shifted the Adirondacks and planters, come inside to nudge the enormous mahogany table an inch, then gone back out, again and again until he had framed it all like one of his pictures. As the sun went down during dinner and the town lights in the valley came up one by one to glisten like seeds of gold in the palm of the land, he had meant for Tessa to feel at peace.

The naked man outside was not a part of that peace.

Bald as a stone and thin as a fir branch, on elbows and knees, he creeps from the neighboring pines like a shaved and emaciated spider. He pauses and shifts to a squat a few feet in from the boundary where natural growth gives way to the lawn's cultivated nudity. The family watches in silence as his long fingers pick at the dirt, sifting between the clipped grass blades. He places a speck of something too small to see in his palm and inspects it closely. He eats it.

Tessa's frail hands shake as she covers her mouth with a red cloth napkin. David places his hand on his sister's chair but stops there. Shara is transfixed, lips moving silently as if counting the man's ribs through his shrink-wrapped skin. Burke and Kels turn to each other with eyes sparkling in code, silently laughing at the same unspoken joke.

"Oh for fuck's sake," Callum grunts. He stomps across the slate floor, rattling the used silverware on finished plates and making the good crystal chirp. He throws open the sliding door and a cool evening breeze runs inside past him. "Hey!" Callum shouts across the lawn. "Hey, you!"

But the man shows no sign of having heard. Still squatting, he runs his fingers through the manicured grass again, as if still searching for the proverbial needle.

From inside, the others watch the disruption through Callum's carefully set frame. He plods across the grass, footprints crushing into the unnatural green. Once Callum is practically on top of him, the thin man looks up from his business in the dirt and his eyes go wide as if in disbelief more than fear.

Now Callum is shouting, pointing at the man, the trees, the lawn. He points to the family inside. Kels waves and Burke hesitates before joining in. The man's eyes open even wider, and he slowly rises as if waking from a dream. Unfolded, he's at least two inches taller than Callum, but no more than a third of his mass. The intruder sways a bit, gangly limbs unsteady.

"Don't do anything stupid," Tessa whispers from her seat, only barely loud enough for David beside her to hear. "Just be—"

The naked man reaches out toward Callum and the family falls silent, all hairs rising in a unison of static. The man places the blackened tips of his thin fingers on Callum's face.

Callum decks him. One punch, felled like a tree.

———

Except for Tessa, who is resting in the deeply cushioned armchair by the empty fireplace, the family stands over the couch where Burke and David have laid the unconscious man on top of a towel from the guest bathroom. Even unfurled here in the living room, the pieces don't quite fit.

Spread out, the man looks so much like a bundle of pine branches that the family can practically smell the resin on him. Up close, they see his scalp is shaved, the hair starting to grow back in needle-sharp tufts. His closed eyes are sunken and his jaw hangs loose where Callum clocked him. His gums have receded so high that his full mouth of yellowed teeth looks like a weathered stone wall. Nevertheless, the slow and almost subterranean depth of his breathing suggests an incongruous peace.

"Where did he come from?" Shara asks.

"Probably crawled out of a hole in the woods," Kels deadpans. None of them are quite sure if she's joking.

"You didn't have to hit him," David says to Callum.

"What was I going to do, David?" Callum tries to maintain a civil tone, but exasperation stretches it at the seams. "Call the cops?"

Silence settles fast on that one. No one's calling the police tonight.

"Still," Tessa finally musters up the strength to say from just outside the circle. "You didn't have to hit him."

Although barely seven o'clock and the fall sun not yet fully set, tonight has clearly been taxing on her. Every night is taxing at this stage of her disease, but even before the intrusion, merely getting *presentable* and holding court with the family was an open drain Callum had been forced to watch his wife pour her last dregs of energy down. She had insisted on it, but now, on the periphery of the group instead of her place of pride at the table's head, Tessa is nearly lost. Her prematurely frail and failing body could almost be an effigy, the vibrant apricot-hued silk of her blouse and matching ochre kerchief with the paisley pattern covering her own nearly bare scalp gleaming like flames about to take her. She looks so tired.

"Tell you what, Tessa," David says loudly, addressing the group through his sister. "Maybe you should rest for a few minutes and catch your breath while we wake this guy up and send him on his way." He beckons to their younger sister: "Kels, can you help Tessa to her room?" To his wife: "Shara, dear?" The women gently hoist Tessa by the arms and then pilot her down the hall toward her ground-floor bedroom.

Once they're gone, David looks to Burke and Callum. "Well? What the hell is this?"

But no one knows. Tramp, tweaker, lunatic, fanatic? Ideas flit about and are swatted down like gnats, but the naked body bears no hint of identification, other than the marks of a nearly ascetic deprivation.

Callum is the first to ask how long the man might have been out there. Images come to him of the naked interloper sneaking around the lodge for days, even before the rest of the family arrived. Watching from the woods and leering at Callum and his wife framed in the lit windows at night. Peeping in from outside, hidden in the shadows, even as Callum had been preparing.

"Cal?" David intrudes into his thoughts. "Are you listening?"

"Sorry." Callum shakes his head. "What?"

"I said, weeks, possibly months," Burke repeats. "Maybe longer? I mean, just look at him."

The man's soles are crusted solid with dirt; his knees and elbows so calloused from crawling that the thick horns of skin resemble plates of bark. And his hands. Spread like a wolf spider's legs, his fingertips are blackened and nails broken so that the ends resemble struck matches. The memory of their stiff yet gummy touch on Callum's cheek begins to draw up a shudder, but he tamps it down. Still, fingers to his own face, there's a ghost of sticky residue.

The men are still circled when Shara and Kels rejoin. Shara sidles up to her husband and rubs his arm, nuzzling against his shoulder. Kels answers Callum's question before he can ask—"She's all right, just resting for a bit"—and then rejoins Burke.

"Well?" Kels asks.

Burke answers: "We were just trying to figure out who this guy is."

"And?"

The men collectively shrug.

After a moment of silence, David asks the obvious question. "Well, what do we do with him? We can't just let him go."

"I don't see why not," Shara says.

David frowns. "He could be a danger to himself."

"Or us," Burke adds, and Kels nods. "Mostly us," they say in unison.

The others turn to David out of habit, but he turns to his brother-in-law. "It's your place, Cal. What do you want to do?"

Before he can answer, though, Shara mutters, "We already know Cal can't wait to push him out to wander off and die. Hands off is his answer to everything."

Callum winces like a bone from deep inside his body has been yanked out from between his ribs. Shara is as deep into her feelings as her cups, but the stench of her words hangs over the naked man's body. David mutters something about "not being fair" while Kels and Burke are silent, and Shara's ears burn claret red as she opens her purple lips again as if maybe to apologize, but Callum doesn't wait to hear it.

"The woodshed. We'll put him there," he says quietly. The rest of the family looks at him, but he can read their minds. "Just until morning. Then someone can take him down the mountain."

Down the mountain, back to the land of the living.

———

Still unconscious, David and Burke lay the naked man down onto the guest towel on the storage shed's dirt floor. The nights get chilly this time of year, so they cover him with the Seahawks fleece from the couch. At Kels's insistence, they also leave him a plastic two-liter bottle filled with tap water like one would a drunk. Afterward, they seal the shed up with the padlock whose combination the whole family knows: Tessa's birthday. Six months to the day from today, as had seemed fitting back when this outing was planned. A day of significance; as far from a birthday as one could get.

The family members regroup in the living room, but with nothing to talk about, they soon disband. Shara, David, and Callum head into the dining room to clean up the remnants of dinner, while Kels and Burke go out for a smoke. Normally David would insist Kels and her boyfriend do the menial work, but tonight Shara shoos them away, seemingly glad for the distraction.

After some inconsequential chatter around the tidying, David asks: "So, what are we going to do about Tessa?"

Shara picks up her glass of Montepulciano which had been left orphaned after the disturbance. She swirls it around, takes a sniff, drains it. "We should put it off," she says while she clears the plates.

"We're not putting it off." Callum shakes his head. "We have a plan."

"But the plan was for this to be a happy time," David says. Shara snorts from over by the sink, but David ignores it.

"Get everyone together," he continues. "Have a nice weekend, a lovely dinner, then—"

Shara drops a handful of silverware into the sink and the clatter cuts David off. Afterward he can't quite bring himself to finish.

Callum takes a deep breath. He closes his eyes and pulls his chin back like he always does when he's upset. "We're still doing that."

"Cal, dear," Shara tries to begin, her voice sweetened by wine or perhaps regret at having suggested he was a killer by neglect, but Callum opens his eyes.

"Look," he says, voice strained nearly to cracking as he slowly points his finger at his in-laws as if to skewer them in place. "Everyone together." Then he sweeps his arms with restrained violence above the table. "Lovely dinner. And then—" He points toward the back of the house where Tessa waits and opens his mouth wide to say the final step, but then closes it and lowers his arms.

"We have a plan," he repeats.

David, ever the professor, sighs in the way that signals a lecture is coming. "Cal, this whole thing is strange, okay? Unusual, let's call it. And I've—we've—been willing to go along with it because it's what she says she wants, but this... For god's sake, Cal, we have a naked man locked in a shed. What are we going to tell Tessa?"

"Maybe it's a sign?" Shara offers.

"It's not a sign," Callum says, "and *you* don't have to tell Tessa anything. I'll tell her it's been handled and that we're all going out to sit around the fire pit and look up at the stars and end the evening, just as we planned. And if you two can just keep your mouths shut for—"

A frenzied rapping on the sliding glass door makes everyone jump. There's a brief moment of panic, but then, through the overlay of the bright interior painted on the glass against the darkness outside, Kels and Burke are on the porch. Kels knocks again and Shara moves in quick, small steps to unlock the door. A troupe of moths fly in behind the couple, hurling their dusty bodies against the nearest bulbs.

Burke and Kels have the resinous and burnt perfume of marijuana around them, and Callum briefly wonders if they brought it or if Tessa has slipped her younger sister her prescription stash. That would be Tessa for you. But then Burke, eyes shining and face glowing from exertion, says, "He's gone."

Kels is nodding vigorously. "So gone."

"Who's gone?" David asks, but they all know who.

"We looked through the window," Kels continues, "but it's closed and the door's still locked."

"So locked," Burke adds.

Callum is already rushing out the side door even as the rest of the family are pulling on windbreakers and flannels from the rack by the front. Outside in short sleeves, his breath fogs in an unseasonable chill as he hoofs it to the shed.

"Goddam it," he hisses with a geyser's steaming spray as he fumbles with the lock. The rest of them are behind him when he opens the door, but Kels and Burke were right—the shed is empty. Well, not entirely. There's a hole in the dirt floor.

No more than twenty inches in diameter, loose soil and rocks are piled up around the rim like an enormous mole's tunnel. Peering in, Callum can see that it doesn't descend straight down but slopes away, making the depth and distance impossible to judge. From here, it doesn't angle toward the western cliff face, but instead back toward the deep heart of the mountain. The same direction as the house.

———

Tessa's bedroom window is fully open, the linen curtain trembling in a frigid breeze. When Callum sticks his head outside and pans across the ground with the emergency flashlight from the kitchen, another hole like the one from the shed yawns beneath the window. The empty mouth seems to whisper: *Let her go.*

David, Shara, Kels, and Burke are crowded by the bedroom doorway, penning Callum in. They begin to chatter while he starts to go through his and Tessa's bags.

"Now we should call the cops," Shara says.

"They won't get here in time," David says. "We have to—"

"What are we going to do?" Kels asks. "Go looking for her in the woods?" She snorts at this.

Burke just stares at the open window. "I'm freaking out, man," he says.

"Cal," David says, trying to get his attention. "Callum. Hey, we— What are those?" He points to the first of the full orange prescription bottles that Cal has put on the bedside table. Then another.

"What do you think they are?" Callum says without turning around. He places another three beside them, five total.

Shara steps forward and picks one up, giving it a rattlesnake shake. She glances at the name, then proceeds to read out the prescription label's directions: "Just before ingestion, dissolve powder from one-hundred capsules into a warm liquid and drink as a single dose."

"One hundred? I thought it was, like, one pill," Kels says.

"Nope," Callum says. "Nothing that simple."

"And she's supposed to do all that prep, cutting open all those tiny pills—"

"No," Callum says. "I'm supposed to do it. I do whatever—" He stops himself. From inside the suitcase, he pulls out a small, locked case and spins the tumblers to a date everyone can guess. The pistol he takes out is sleek and new; only ever fired at the range to make sure it works and won't jam. With unsure hands, he removes the magazine to confirm it's loaded, reminds himself where the safety mechanism is, then reloads it. He stands up, gun in hand, and turns to find the rest of the family staring at him.

"Cal," Kels says, "why do you have that gun?"

His hand trembles up and down as if it were a scale taking the weight.

"Protection," he says, but everyone knows he's lying.

"C'mon, Cal," David says, slowly approaching with a hand stretched out. "I know things have been really difficult, but let's just go and call the police, okay? You can put that away and we'll let the professionals handle it."

"No!" Cal snaps. "Tessa is my responsibility. I'm not going to let her—" He flinches at the near-slip. "Not out there. Not scared and alone."

"Please," Kels says, joining David with her hand also raised. "Please just calm down."

"Please," Shara says, the bottle of pills still in her hand, rattling as she trembles.

"I am, like, really freaking out," Burke says, red eyes wide.

Tessa's family is circling Callum now like a pack of wolves, but with a sudden jerk, he lunges toward the open window and tumbles out through the narrow opening, onto the ground. When he looks up, all four of them are framed in the window like the annual family portrait. He's behind the camera, as always, only this time there's no Tessa there to connect him to the other side. They are waiting for him to push the button, for the flash, for him to disappear.

Gun and flashlight in hand, Callum scrambles arms first into the hole that stole his wife, wriggling his way deep into the dirt and down into the mountain.

———

The tunnel opens up as the burrowed soil's floor descends sharply to connect with a more permanent path carved through the rock itself. The walls are smooth as river stones here, and Callum can raise himself up from his belly to his hands and knees. He tucks the pistol in the back of his waistband and crawls onward with the flashlight pointed ahead, its yellow eye of light bobbing up and down, fading into the darkness.

Smaller capillary passages branch off the arterial tunnel at irregular intervals. Shrinking, they twist and wind away, whatever secrets they hold resting outside of the curious flashlight's beam. If the naked man has taken Tessa down one of these paths, Callum has no way to tell. Instead, it's a matter of gravity if not faith that pulls him onward down the main tunnel until he reaches the fork.

Two branches diverge, both of seemingly equal size and level slope, neither with any overt markings to recommend one over the other. He pauses there and turns off the flashlight, hoping for something, anything to guide him: a sound, a movement of the air, a faint gleam of light. Anything.

But all he hears is the rush of blood through the tubes in his own ears; all he feels is the hammer of his heart; and all he sees are the negative-space dots that swim before his blinded eyes under the exertion.

And then there is something else. The tunnel on the right: a faint gleam, just enough so that the quality of darkness is slightly less, even though the quantity is not. And is that a faint sound, like a far-off moaning? It's so minimal that it bobs in and out of the waves of tinnitus in Callum's ears, but it's definitely there. That decides it. He flips the flashlight on and, with a renewed vigor, presses forward down the rightmost tunnel, heading to rescue Tessa.

Time and distance have little meaning in the underground, but the distant glow begins to draw closer. Callum turns off the flashlight again and, yes, the blackness at the tunnel's end has faded now to a deep bathyal blue. The sound of intermittent moaning is clearer, too, but unlike any he has ever heard—it is almost spectral, quivering through the tunnel. Leaving the flashlight off for the element of surprise, he pushes forward, the open mouth of an entrance growing closer and closer until, with one final turn, he is there.

The tunnel dead ends in a small chamber the size of the mountain lodge's half-bath. Bored from the rock in the same smooth fashion as the tunnel, there is a fissure in the stone ceiling and roots from above spread it open like fingers in a wound to let in the barest hint of light. The dim illumination gives the room a submarine quality: the hint of blue; the twinkling flecks of mica and glowing thumbs of pink crystal embedded in the abyssal walls like schools of mineral fish. An incongruous scent of spice permeates the still air, seeming to rise from clay jars that sit along the walls, but especially from the deep reef of shadows pooling on the bundled mound of green cloth and sticks and stones in the room's center.

Callum flicks on the flashlight and gasps. The mass before him has a face like weathered leather, frozen in a rictus grin. The roots descending from the broken roof rest gentle centipede tendrils across the bare scalp, crawling over it with many slow fingers. For a moment Callum tries to convince himself it must be a mask or prop, but the faint weeds of eyebrows and lashes around the empty sockets and the needle-sharp tufts of hair on the parchment scalp tell the truth. The broad yellow teeth smile behind lips puckered like a beak.

The mummified body sits cross-legged, the simple elegance of its emerald robes desaturated by a fine film of dust that gathers in the folds and along the edges of the vine-like embroidery on the hems and lapel. Its hands lay upright in its lap, and Callum recognizes the long, tapered fingers, stained black at the ends. While this desiccated corpse before him is not the naked man, it could as well be a brother or a sister.

The wind above ground must blow, for the moaning from the mouth of stone above him intensifies, and the tree growing above must shudder, too, because the roots move. Under their caress, the body shivers as if waking up to Callum's intrusion. It is time for him to leave.

Squeezing himself as small as possible, Callum maneuvers into turning around. Leaving his back exposed gives him a chill, so he scuttles quickly down to where the main arterial path had branched. Now at the intersection again, the slow realization creeps up on him that the entire mountain must be a warren of tunnels like an ant colony, each cell at the end of each branching finger housing a dead man or woman who has chosen to linger on in this secret half-decay until the end of time. Holy or terrible, he doesn't know, but the magnitude of the revelation has shaken him—the irony of his days spent blithely eating and sleeping over this midden of hidden bodies; carrying on in his petty life, all the while suspended above these macabre relics stretching their frozen ends out into eternity—and now that he has fully crossed the border into the Land of *Die*, he wants nothing more than to leave.

But Callum can't.

————

Callum can't recall the exact shape of his and Tessa's long road to this mountain top, but he remembers the moment when the mists parted and he could finally see where their path was leading. He remembers the exact instant when more than the *idea* of it—more even than the *knowledge* of it—the *belief* of it struck him. The moment when the film reel of their life together snagged in the projector and everything that was meant to come after started spooling out, heaps of still images tumbling into a pile of celluloid garbage.

Hadn't he done everything he was supposed to?

Because for months before that moment, it seemed like all there was to do was fight it. Every word out of Callum's mouth was a variation on the theme: *fight this together, keep fighting, don't give up the fight.* But as round after round drew to a close, Tessa grew bruised and irritable beneath the uncertainty of what pain each new day and each new test would bring. Although he could not say it, Callum, too, grew more and more skittish, until every shadow seemed cast by indifferent cosmic dice tumbling down to crush them.

Perhaps each saw it as their duty to carry the other? Was that what locked them into the push and pull until every waking moment between them seemed to chafe, their tears of anger or frustration an inadequate balm?

Until one night, when he came home late from his studio to find her sitting at the kitchen table with an untouched glass of water before her, eyes closed and still as a saint in a glass coffin. Already, when the light was too direct, her skin sagged from the architecture of bone beneath, and seeing her, the blood in his heart thickened like sap.

He had stopped by the grocery store as a way to further delay returning and picked up a bouquet of white Crème de la crème roses and fluffy fingers of lavender from the baskets by the automatic door. But when Tessa took them from him in both hands, tendons straining like cables through the thin skin while she forced a smile, the bouquet looked positively funereal. He took them back, muttering something about putting them in a vase.

"How was your day?" he asked as he puttered through the cabinets with one hand. He heard her chair scoot across the tile to make space, but she didn't rise.

"Callum," Tessa began, and the use of his full name stopped him. "It's time to start discussing the other possibilities."

"But, Tess," he said, hands crushing the fragile green stems without attention, "you don't want... Don't you want—"

"Honey, no," she interrupted. "I love you, but no more fighting."

That was the moment. The film caught. Everything still to come began smoking, melting.

And soon after, it was Doctor Wells who was the first to say in front of Callum that Tessa was going to *die*. Not *pass on*, not *pass over*, not *be at rest*, but *die*. Callum had hated that woman so much it burned.

Doctor Wells was older than them by only about a decade, well-credentialed and discretely recommended, but the words she used were profanity: *die, death, dying, dead*. Again and again, she threw them out—not casually, but each one direct and pointed. Their barbed tips stuck like a picador's javelins, wounding and weighing Callum down until he wanted nothing more than to bellow and charge across the consultation room to gore the ghoul in white telling them that his Tessa would be *dead.*

He wanted to scream. He wanted to curse, but what good were *fuck, shit,* or *damn* in the Land of *Die?*

And so, Callum would stare at himself in the mirror at home, in the hospital bathroom, in his car, and say the words over and over again like a mantra: "Tessa is *dying.* My wife is going to *die.* My best friend will be *dead.*"

There was nothing they could do to avoid it, only nudge the arc of the experience.

———

Outside on the mountain face, a storm must be coming because now every path off the main tunnel groans as if rising from sleep, their spiced breath of incense and curing agents wafting down into the main tube. The mountain is singing a dirge, its myriad stone throats trembling like a choir that hungers to swallow the world in ten thousand bites. For Tessa, though, Callum pushes on into the gut of the mummified empire.

At last, the tunnel opens into a central chamber the size of the mountain home's living room. Inside, a burning brazier paints the walls red and orange, the glowing seeds of charcoal pulsating with each breath of wind from the seven openings spaced at equal intervals in the round wall. Yet the unexpected warmth is welcome, and the chamber is tall enough for Callum to stand, at least. His aching limbs thank and curse him in equal measure as he rises.

A handful of ceramic jars squat along the walls; a worn reed mat with a neatly folded set of empty brick-red robes sits in the middle. There is no corpse here—mummified or not—but the room is otherwise as spartan as the previous cell. Well, not entirely. There's a small, crumpled object on the floor by one of the far tunnels.

Drawing nearer, the swirls and shadows resolve into the folds of a discarded cloth. Callum stoops to pick it up, and the cool silk between his fingertips and paisley pattern swimming in the dim light confirm: this is Tessa's kerchief. He recalls how she had spent so long selecting the matching ensemble of flame-colored blouse and scarf especially for this evening that, weakened by the effort, she'd had to ask Callum to tie it over her almost-naked scalp. The sensation of pulling the knot echoes through the nerves of his fingers.

Then the sounds of a slow, approaching shuffle roll out from the tunnel ahead and Callum's heart begins to race. He steps back. With shaking hands, he draws the pistol and tries to steady his aim on the dark and open mouth. Tessa's orange kerchief dangles from his hand like a foxtail and he says a silent prayer to a god he hates, the bitter confection of the words like burnt sugar on his still tongue.

The thin, naked man emerges from the tunnel on all fours. Unfolding himself as he enters the chamber, he is even taller, even thinner than he was outside. Here in the red and orange light, head scraping the stone ceiling, he towers like a burning pine. Then he sees Callum and fixes his sunken eyes on the intruder. His long hands with the fingertips like charcoal hang at his side.

"Don't move," Callum says. "Or I'll kill you."

The words echo through the chamber and out into the tunnels, each repetition growing softer, less substantial, until there's nothing left but the distant wind. The threat of death rings hollow in the Land of *Die*.

Now, with their places from the world above reversed, it is Callum who stares with dreamy wonder as the strange man before him approaches. He moves with uncanny grace, the awkwardness from the sunlit world above now shed and the shadows of his ribs striping him like a tiger in the brazier's light.

Callum pulls the pistol's trigger, but the trigger refuses to budge. He squeezes again and again in futile repetition, realizing too late that the safety is still engaged. But by then the man is close enough that Callum can smell the spice rising from his skin, its pungent immediacy transcending the coal smoke. Then the man is reaching out with those sharp, black fingers, and Callum cannot move or look away.

But the man does not touch Callum or the gun. Instead, the tips of his fingers graze Tessa's kerchief, still dangling from Callum's hand. The silk moves like the curtain from her bedroom, and with a gentle pressure, the man tugs on it as if to free it, but Callum will not let go. Undeterred, the stranger begins to back away, pulling the kerchief like a leash toward the tunnel he just crawled out from. Callum hesitates, but the man crooks one darkened finger and beckons: *Come.*

In an instant, Callum can envision the man outside of Tessa's bedroom window. Where he had previously imagined her being pulled out and dragged down in a funnel web spider's gaunt embrace, he now envisions only a single long finger gesturing for her to follow. He imagines her climbing out slowly and following the man into the tunnels.

Callum allows himself to be pulled toward the mouth of the passage.

When they reach the opening, the man lets go of the silken tether and points up into the tunnel. *Up there*, he seems to say, and Callum's vision shifts again. He no longer sees Tessa trailing the man into the tunnel, caught in his thrall. Instead, he sees her clear as day, watching as the man points into the hole, pointing to the thing she wanted most of all—the Land of *Die.* He sees Tessa kneeling down to lead the way.

Callum returns the faithless pistol to the back of his waistband and joins the tall man. Up close, he can see that the tight skin drawn across the man's jawline bears no blemish from where Callum struck him. While recognition glints in the man's eyes, there is no ember of anger or ill will, but nor is there any suggestion of warmth or affection. What has happened is not a good thing or a bad thing, his smooth face seems to say. This is just how it is in the mountain.

Beneath the incense and charcoal and mineral odors of the chamber, there is the hint of another scent wafting down the tunnel. A whiff of white roses and lavender. He can see Tessa, buried in flowers, eyes closed, waiting.

Callum nods slowly to the man, then kneels down to crawl into darkness after her.

———

Earlier that afternoon, once the sun had crested the peak and only just begun its descent, the mountain lodge was in the path of direct light. Just hours ago, Tessa had been resting by the living room's picture window, Kels and Shara sitting beside her, the soft sounds of their idle chatter carrying through the lodge to where Callum had been fussing with the arrangements for dinner. It had to be perfect.

"You should go and spend time with her," David said in a low voice from the dining room's doorway. He gestured to the tableau. "This is all fine. It's good enough."

But it wasn't. It would never be good enough. If there was one thing Callum knew from his art, it was that nothing was ever *finished*—only at a stage where it could or must be abandoned. This wasn't that. Not yet.

"I just need some more time," he said. Looking out the glass door, the chair on the porch was crooked from this angle and would need to be fixed. The pots of purple catmint and orange sunset blanket flowers could also be better balanced.

David pouted. "Callum, there are only hours left. Don't you want to spend every moment with her that you can?"

But David couldn't guess at all the moments Callum had already spent with Tessa. David hadn't been with them for the tests, the pain. The messes. The tears. He and the others had joined them for the last hurrah, the *bon voyage*, at Tessa's request, but Callum was exhausted.

He shook his head. "I just want it to be over, okay?"

David furrowed his brow. "What's that supposed to mean?"

"Nothing, David. I'm just ready to be done."

"So what?" David asked. "Tessa—my sister—she just, just..." But he couldn't bring himself to say the word. "She just *passes on*, and then what?"

The phrase made it sound like a boat trip. Like they were seeing her off but that soon she'd disembark with her steamer trunk on the other side and call to let them know she'd made it safely. It was all so tiring. No postcards were coming from the Land of *Die*.

"Then what?" David repeated.

"Then she's *dead*," Callum said, giving the word a granite weight, sinking the pleasure cruise of *passes on* beneath the boulder. "*Nothing* comes after. That's the end."

But that was too much. Callum could see something drowning in David's eyes. All his life of being the older brother, all his education, his lectures, his money, and it would all sink down into nothing. Just nothing.

"Then why are you in such a hurry?" David whispered.

In a flash, Callum could see that David's fear was a connection they shared, and that David himself was a connection—no matter how thin—that Callum could use to hold on to Tessa even after she swallowed the final dose this evening and drifted off into sleep under the stars. She was supposed to find sleep in minutes, then death in hours, but it was Callum's duty to see it through and bear watch until the very end. It was a burden that surely her brother must understand.

"Because honestly, David, I can't keep it together much longer," Callum confided softly, "and I don't want the last thing Tessa sees to be me going to pieces. I want this to be as easy as possible."

But whatever cord Callum thought he and David might share snapped, the broken ends whipping through the air. "Easy for who?" David sneered, the whispers dropped. "Why should this be easy for you?" He shook his head in exaggerated disappointment, a trick that worked on his students and possibly his sisters, but a mistake to deploy against Callum. Not tonight.

There was so little that Callum had control over, so why couldn't David let him have just this one thing? Callum had spent time with Tessa, so much time that was all at once too much and yet could never, ever, ever be enough. Why couldn't David and the rest of them just let Callum deal with his grief in his own way for just one hour—to take a few steps back from the Land of *Die* and just set a goddamn table and frame a final picture for his wife? To catch his own breath before their last night together? That's what he had wanted to say.

But he had never been good at communicating with her family.

"Because, you stupid asshole," Callum said far too loudly, "I'm the one who has to do it all, and when the love of my life is fucking *dead*, I'm the one who's going to be left."

Out in the living room, the echoes of chatter fell silent. The whole house was silent.

"Jesus," David said. "Okay." He backed away, still shaking his head as he retreated to the living room. "Hey, sis," he greeted Tessa at a performative volume. "How are you feeling?"

The murmurs resumed, but Callum knew that Tessa had heard him. Everyone on the mountain had heard him. And as surely as if his words had been a spell that summoned the stranger from the pines and scooped out the holes that had swallowed Tessa, Callum knew that he had driven her down into the mountain.

————

The end of the tunnel ahead glows with an almost emerald hue, the color of grass or moss after a rain. As Callum approaches, however, the stone walls constrict, squeezing him down until he crawls on his elbows, then slides on his belly. It becomes harder to breathe, pressed on all sides, and he has to back up enough to work the gun out from his waistband and the flashlight from his pocket in order to leave them behind so that he can fit through ahead. Naked without his last protections, he tucks Tessa's orange kerchief down into his shirt and crawls further into the flesh of the mountain.

Closer now. Almost there. The scope of the tunnel frames the room before him and Tessa is sitting there in the middle of the mats, now clad in orange robes like pajamas, propped up on faded pillows. Her eyes are closed, lips pursed but jaw slack. In the dim storm-green light which oozes from a hole in the stone ceiling, her thin shoulders don't appear to move. With an anguished howl, he struggles forward to grasp for her, but his fingers can only just graze the embroidered flames on the linen hem of her orange robes. It is always too little, too late.

"Cal?"

He looks up, and Tessa is staring down at him. His body tries to heave a sob, but with most of him still pinned in the tunnel, he can only grunt. "Hi, hon," is all he can manage.

Tessa blinks her eyes as if waking from a slumber. "Oh, Cal," she says. "You aren't supposed to be here."

"I'm always supposed to be with you," he says. Callum works himself out and into the small stone room, kneeling almost on top of her. Tessa lets out a deep breath that stirs the scent of incense and lavender, and Callum can't help but notice that her fingers are tinged with a faint purple, the tips so inky as to be almost black. She raises a thin hand to Callum's face and, unwittingly, he flinches.

But no. This is the woman he loves. Thinner, yes, and bones closer to the surface, but the familiar warmth and tenderness radiates within. He relaxes into her.

But then she withdraws, and the sudden coolness on his cheek from the absence sickens him. The gun calls to him from the tunnel, whispering that there's a way they can stay together under the mountain forever.

"I'm sorry," he says, meaning everything.

"It's okay," she replies, and he knows she means the same. "This isn't your fault, it's just what's happening." She pauses. "I can't change that I'm dying, Cal. I can only control how I do. But..."

She trails off, but Callum can imagine what she's going to say. She's going to say that even then it isn't fully her choice how this happens. The hoops she jumped through to get the necessary medical assistance were onerous enough, but the added pressures of the family? The pressures of her husband? All these things to consider when she should be able to just focus on herself?

"We shouldn't have invited the others—"

"I wanted them," Tessa says, but then corrects herself. "Well, not Burke, necessarily. Do you remember how many nice young men I've tried to set Kelly up with?" She tuts lightly. "She could do so much better."

Callum can't help but smile, even though it feels wrong. "You know they say the same about you and me."

"Pfaw." She flutters her hand. "You're different."

"If he makes her happy, though, isn't that enough?"

"I suppose," Tessa says, and slips into a wistful smile. "What are they going to do without me?"

"Fall to pieces, at first," he says. "But then they'll think of what you would have done, and they'll be all right."

"I hope so," she says, but then her face tautens, and the moment of levity is gone. "And you, my love? What are you going to do without me?"

Again, he hears the gun whisper from the tunnel. He doesn't say anything, but Tessa could always read his mind.

"Honey," she says. "This is a place you come when it's your time."

"But it doesn't have to be your time," he says. "We could keep—"

She places a single darkened finger against his lips and the scent of wild-flowers silences him. "We said we wouldn't fight. I've made my choice."

Gently, Callum pulls her finger away. Tears enough to drown them both are threatening to burst free, but only a single one manages to escape, which he thumbs quickly from his cheek. "Aren't you scared?" he asks.

"No," Tessa says without hesitation. "Not for myself."

"But for me," Callum says, and it's not a question.

"Cal." Tessa rubs her thin fingers over the back of his hand, his wrist. "You don't have to be here. I worry that I've been selfish, and I don't want to make you watch as I stop breathing, wondering if each one will be the last until I leave you forever waiting for the one that never comes. And I...well, I don't want to drift off into my final dream knowing that I've caused you unnecessary pain." She closes her eyes and lets the fingers tracing her husband's wrist fall limp. "I was hoping this would be easier."

Callum turns his hand over, and hers slips in to meet him palm-to-palm. They squeeze one another, and the pressure of their buried strength together wrings fresh rivulets of tears from Callum's eyes, but this time he lets them stay.

"I don't want *easier*," he says. "I want to be with you. And whether it's here, up there, or anywhere, I want to be at your side when it's your time to —" But now that it is here before them, he can no longer say it. He tries again: "When you—" But he can't.

Tessa opens her eyes again and there is the flash of crystal-clear truth, burning like a flame too bright as it runs between them like a fire through the pines, burning out all the old growth in the Land of *Die*. It sears the brook of his tears away, evaporating them like the morning sun upon the dew as she leans into him and presses her burning lips to his.

"It's okay," Tessa whispers.

"I love you." Callum swallows. "I want to be with you until you die."

"I know," she says. "Me too."

———

———

———

The sun rises in the east, behind the mountain home, and the shadow of the peak leaves the view from the dining room shrouded in half-light like a fog as morning breaks. David is the first one up, stumbling into the unfamiliar kitchen to begin making coffee. As the machine heats up and the percolator begins to boil over, he stretches lazily and glances out over the empty dining room table and toward the sliding glass door.

He looks out and he blinks. Again. There's no mistaking it—Callum is sprawled on his back in the yard, arms spread out as if asking for a final hug from the sky. Beside his prone form, an Adirondack rocker has been dragged across the grass, leaving furrows of torn sod behind it, and in the rocker is a pile of orange blankets. The top of Tessa's paisley apricot kerchief crowns the unmoving mound.

David yells for his family and they stumble ragtag out of their rooms, but one by one, they look out the window and are blown awake.

"Is that?" David asks, pointing to the bundle in the chair beside Callum on the law.

"Is she?" Shara mumbles.

"Is he?" Kels asks.

"What the shit?" Burke gasps.

David fumbles with the sliding door, managing to open it but knocking the screen off the tracks, and the family tumbles over themselves onto the porch and then down onto the grass. Cold crystal tears of dew soak through socks and coat bare feet. Fixated on the still shape swaddled in orange blankets on the Adirondack, they run toward it in slow motion as if frozen in a shared dream.

But Callum is warm. The sun is reaching around the beckoning finger of the peak, the lavender clouds are spreading off into an open horizon, and the birds are beginning to wake and sing. His breath steams as he takes in and releases deep lungfuls of air.

Publication History

"Gordon B. White is creating Haunting Weird Horror" first published in *Nightmare Magazine,* July 2021.

"One of the Good Ones; or, It's a Gas!" first published in *Antifa Splatterpunk* (Cursed Morsels Publishing, 2022).

"Dandelion Six" first published in *Field Notes from a Nightmare* (Dreadstone Press, 2021).

"Godhead" is original to this collection.

"The Forever Home" first published in *The Breakroom Stories* (2018).

"What a Piece of Work" first published in *Boneyard Soup*, Vol. 1, No. 2 (2021).

"The Parts of Him That I Can Help With" first published in *Mad Scientist Journal* (Winter 2019).

"From October Vines" first published in *Weird Horror* No. 3 (Undertow Publications, 2021).

"Fine and Fancy Arms" first published in *A Walk in a Darker Wood* (Alien Sun Press, 2020).

"Paper Wings and Arrow Juice" first published at *Tales to Terrify*, Episode 446 (2020).

Publication History

"A Song Like Laughter" first published in *Tales from Canyons of the Damned*, No. 34 (2019).

"Junippy Paw" first published at *Tales to Terrify*, Episode 510 (2021).

"Hearth and Home" first published in *Home* (Ghost Orchid Press, 2021).

"Devil Take Me" first published in *Nightmare Magazine*, November 2022.

"In the Pines" is original to this collection.

Acknowledgments

As I write this, I can't help but reflect on how the last few years of existence have been, for lack of a better word, trying. My first collection released right before the first lockdown, and while the ensuing years have seen my highest professional highs, they have also occasioned some of my lowest personal lows. Wider reader recognition and awards nominations were incredibly validating, but the shakeup of our previous way of life (especially the isolation) was a massive struggle that I still don't think is over. No amount of publications or plaudits can fix that.

What have I learned? Not much, I'm afraid. At least, no lessons that I'm far enough away from at this point to articulate. Except, maybe, that in life, as well as in art, it helps to find meaning in the process because the product won't save you.

By that, I mean that when I set about compiling this collection of stories that were written both in the Before Times and the Now Times, I was initially skeptical of how they would fit together. But while certain themes and underpinnings may differ from one story to the next, I see within them a joy in the process of writing. I see the love of a particular plot twist or character here; the exhilaration of working within formal constraints there; the enthusiastic embrace of structure one moment and the cautious excitement of delving into unknown the next. No matter when they were written, in these stories I find again and again the thrill of tuning into the creative and mysterious frequencies, encountering and channeling different voices.

Different voices but, in hindsight, all my voice. Hence the title. What unites the stories in this collection are that they were all written by me for the sake of writing to survive. Whether that was early on when I was struggling to find a way to balance the necessity of workaday life with a meaningful creative existence or later on as a way not to crack up as the world seemed to fall apart, these stories in particular come from a real experience of joy in writing, even if the stories themselves aren't necessarily joyful. None of them were written for awards or even necessarily for readers. They were written by and for Gordon B. White, through and for the love of creating haunting weird horror(s).

So yes, I suppose I have learned to find joy and meaning in the process, but not just in writing. It applies to life too, so let me thank some of the people who have helped me in both arenas:

My thanks, of course, to my wife, Casey, and our dog, Saucy. I literally couldn't survive without you. My thanks, too, to my mom and my brother back east, who are as supportive as physical distance allows.

Much thanks to all the editors and outlets who gave these stories their first life, as well as a helpful eye and hand to shape them. Every one of them was a pleasure and a pro, and I'd work with them again as soon as they'll let me.

In particular, my great thanks to Wendy N. Wagner, who has been a fantastic editor and friend. Without her giving "Gordon B. White etc." a chance to find an appreciative audience that grew beyond my wildest expectations, you most certainly would not be reading this book now. At the very least it would be called something different.

My thanks, too, to the writers who are friends and keep me sane through correspondence and the too-rare in-person chat: Clint; Corey; David; Jacob; Keith; and Philip. Also, to the Thursday night co-writing regulars who provide the good kind of peer pressure: Adrian, Brittany, Cat, Christina, Clay, Cynthia, David, Ed, Elly, James, Jo, Jordan, John, Laura, Matt, Mike, Sofia, Steve, Stevie, Tania, Victoria, Wailana, Zach, and everyone else. And a special shout out for my favorite beta reader, Iori, and some helpful spot-checking from Jack Reigns.

I must also give due credit to the team that helps me make these haunting weird horrors into haunting weird books: my publisher, Christopher Payne; my proofreader, Sean Leonard; and my editor and guiding light, Scarlett Algee.

And finally, my sincerest and deepest thanks to the readers. As much as I love the process, knowing that there's someone—anyone—waiting to read more makes it worthwhile. For a collection with a lot of second person stories, believe me when I say that YOU are the most important character.

—*Seattle, WA*

About the Author

Gordon B. White is a Shirley Jackson Award- and Bram Stoker Award-nominated writer of horror and weird fiction. He is the author of the collection *As Summer's Mask Slips and Other Disruptions* (2020), and the novellas *Rookfield* (2021) and *And In Her Smile, the World* (with Rebecca J. Allred, 2022). A graduate of the Clarion West Writing Workshop, Gordon's stories have appeared in dozens of venues, including "best of the year" lists and a Bram Stoker Award® winning anthology. He also contributes reviews and interviews to various genre outlets. You can find him online at www.gordonbwhite.com or on most social media @GordonBWhite.

Printed in the USA
CPSIA information can be obtained
at www.ICGtesting.com
JSHW021029301123
52886JS00004B/94

9 781685 100940